DRAGON TALES

Book IV

The Runaway

For Theo

Judy Hayman.

This is the fourth of the Dragon Tales Chronicles.
Already published:
Dragon Tales Book I: Quest for a Cave
Dragon Tales Book II: Quest for a Friend
Dragon Tales Book III: Quest for Adventure

Coming soon:
Dragon Tales Book V: Dragons in Snow
The Dragon Tales Colouring Book

DRAGON TALES

BOOK IV

The Runaway

by

Judy Hayman

illustrated by

Caroline Wolfe Murray

Practical Inspiration
PUBLISHING

First published in Great Britain by Practical
Inspiration Publishing, 2015

© Judy Hayman 2015
All illustrations by Caroline Wolfe Murray
The moral rights of the author and illustrator have
been asserted.

ISBN (print): 978-1-910056-28-8
ISBN (ebook): 978-1-910056-27-1

This one is for Megan, who writes good Dragon
stories and helps me with mine.
J.L.H.

For Matthew, Lucy, Rebecca and Emily.
C.W.M.

Table of contents

Chapter 1

Secret Plans

T om and Ollie were hiding in their tree-house. It was a bit of a ramshackle affair, just a small shoogly platform and a screen of pine branches wedged into the fork of an elderly oak. It had only one advantage. Nobody else ever wanted to sit in it.

If they peered through the gaps in the walls they could just see another tree-house – a much more splendid creation. That one had taken many days to build, and everyone had helped, even the grown-ups. It was halfway up the biggest oak in their patch of woodland and not too close to the camp by the loch that Ollie's family had set up in the early summer. It had a proper floor, and walls with windows and a flat branch for landing on, so you could fly up and enter without an undignified scramble through the branches.

Unfortunately it also belonged to the girls!

While the building was in progress, the four young dragons had worked together quite well. On fine days, Tom and his older sister Emily had flown over from their cave on the hill and they had worked hard at the building. On wet days Ollie and Alice had visited the cave, and they had drawn elaborate plans on smooth bits of Emily's bedroom wall. There had been a good deal of arguing of course, but no real fights. In the cave, Ollie and Tom could always move into Tom's room, to make wild plans of their own, but in the finished tree-house, there was nowhere to plan in secret.

The four had spent most of the morning arguing about whose turn it was to fetch fresh heather for seats (and sometimes beds), and finally the boys had left and hidden up their own tree, feeling thoroughly fed up.

It was the middle of September, and there was a feeling of autumn in the air. The nights were getting longer, and round the fire, as the stars came out, the grown-ups had been talking about the coming winter. Unfortunately, nobody ever asked the youngsters for their opinion!

The winter had never been a problem to Tom and Emily and their parents. They were used to cold weather

2

in the Scottish Highlands. Even now they had a new baby, little golden Lily, to look after, they could stock their roomy cave with stores of food and firewood and snuggle down in shelter through the worst of the weather. But Ollie and Alice had never lived in a cave. Their family had travelled a lot, and had always flown south for the winter. They had never lived so long in one place before. They had enjoyed their summer in the Highlands, living near to another dragon family with very little risk of discovery by Humans, but their woodland camp would be of little use in the snow.

Tom was depressed at the thought of losing Ollie, and he knew – though they never talked about it – that Emily felt the same about Alice. He could remember living in their old cave, and Emily talking on and on about how she would love to have a friend. It was because of this longing that they had managed to find Ollie and his family and bring them up to live by the second loch. Deep down, Tom knew that he had Emily to thank for his friend Ollie, but, being a little brother, he would never dream of telling her so!

He was just about to propose a swim in the loch to try to cheer Ollie up, when he caught a whiff of

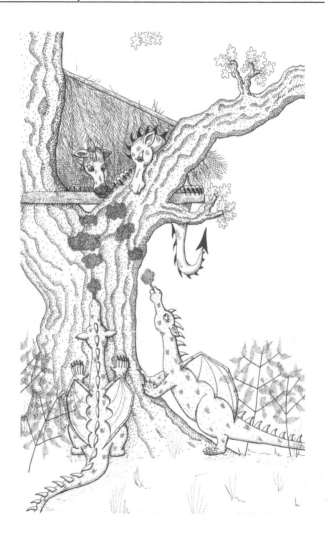

smoke drifting up past the branches of their hiding place. He nudged Ollie and they both peered down. At the foot of the tree Emily and Alice were huffing smoke up the trunk towards them.

Ollie scowled. "Peace or war?" he said.

Alice rolled her eyes in exasperation. "Peace! We want to talk to you."

"You can come up if you like," Tom offered.

"No thanks," said Emily. "You come to ours. There's more room. We have bumbugs and ginger fizz," she added, knowing Tom's weakness.

The boys exchanged glances. "OK," said Ollie, "but no kids allowed." He hated having to look after Lily or his own little brother Georgie.

"Just us," Alice agreed, "a council of war!"

The two boys climbed awkwardly through the branches and launched themselves to the ground, trying to ignore the superior smirks of the girls as they landed in a tangle of tails and wings.

They decided to creep through the bushes round the back of the camp instead of flying, as there was less chance of being spotted by Georgie. Then one by one, they flew up to the landing branch and scrambled inside. Emily, the last, pulled the bracken door shut behind them.

"Do sit down," said Alice politely, pointing to the neat piles of new dry heather on the floor.

"This is our place as well," Ollie pointed out grumpily, but he and Tom sat down as Emily brought mugs of ginger fizz and placed a pile of stripy bumblebugs on a large dock leaf on the floor between them.

"Right," said Alice. "I suppose we all know that Mum and Dad are thinking of leaving for the winter. They don't think we can survive up here in the woods."

"We manage," said Tom. "It's not that bad. It's great when it snows!"

"We've got a cave," said Emily. "I wouldn't like to spend the winter in the open. But couldn't you come and share our cave in the worst of the weather?"

"It's too small," said Ollie, sounding suddenly grown up and sensible. "Remember that night we all stayed during the thunderstorm? You could hardly move! I think Grandad is the main problem.

He wasn't very well last winter, and we lived down south where there was hardly any snow. Then there's Georgie. I can see why Mum and Dad think we should leave, though I don't particularly want to. This is the best place we've ever lived in!" Alice nodded agreement.

Tom felt very downcast. "It'll be awfully boring with just Emily."

Emily refused to quarrel. Things were far too serious. She was very fond of Old George, Alice's grandfather, and couldn't bear the thought that he might get ill over the winter. She suddenly had an idea. "There's our old cave!" she exclaimed. "It's not that far away. It's a bit small, but if you're only there for a few weeks it might do. Perhaps they'd let you two stay with us – that'd leave more room. Let's see what they say!"

She was so excited by her idea that she got up ready to fly down and suggest it right away, but for once it was Tom who thought of a snag.

"What about the Humans?" he said.

"Were there Humans there?" Alice sounded shocked.

"No, but they were starting to build further down the glen," Emily explained. "That's why we came here. But we don't *know* that they've found our old cave. It was quite a long way up the glen. Dad said the place would soon be overrun with Humans, but he was probably exaggerating."

"There's only one way to find out," said Ollie. "We'll have to go and see!"

"We'd never be allowed."

"Of course we wouldn't! But if we say we're just going for a flight and a picnic in the hills, they won't know. Then we'll fly as fast as we can to your old cave. We're all strong flyers since we came back from that trip to the sea with Des, and we've had a decent rest since then. We'll be late back and get into a row, but by then we'll have found out what we need to know. Then we just need to talk the parents round." Ollie sounded so confident that even Alice, who was usually the most responsible of the four, was persuaded.

"Are you sure you know the way?" she asked Emily.

"I think so," said Emily, sounding just a little worried. "It would be easier from our cave than from here. A bit nearer too. We'll ask if you can spend the night with us and then we can get a really early start."

"The day after tomorrow," Ollie decided. "That'll give us time to get things ready. How about a swim before you have to go home?"

Feeling a good deal more cheerful, they shared out the last of the bumblebugs, squeezed one by one through the doorway and took off from the landing branch.

At the side of the loch they found little Georgie playing in the shallows watched over by Old George. He was whirling round in circles, sweeping the water with his tail and flapping his wings.

George waved as they came in to land.

"I saw you come out of the tree-house together," he said, pleased. "That must mean the latest quarrel is over?"

"Suppose so," said Tom, following Ollie into the deeper water. They both dived and disappeared.

"Allie, Allie!" shouted Georgie, and Alice waded in to rescue her little brother as he tripped and fell, spluttering, into the water. Emily sat down beside George and heaved a heavy sigh.

"You'll miss Alice when we have to leave," he said sympathetically. Emily looked up into his wise kindly face and wished she could tell him about their plan. Even though it had been partly her idea, she couldn't help worrying. What if she couldn't find the way after all? What if they found that Humans had discovered the cave already? No, she couldn't ask his advice. He would be bound to tell their parents and then they'd never be allowed to go.

She forced herself to smile at him. "Of course I will," she said. "I'll miss all of you, even Ollie. But you'll come back when the winter's over. And you never know – you may not have to go at all!"

She got up and splashed her way into the loch to help Alice, who was giving Georgie a ride into the deeper water.

George watched her go, and heaved a sigh of his own. "Oh, I think we will...." he said sadly to himself.

Chapter 2

Back to the Old Cave

It was very early in the morning when the four young dragons set off on their expedition. Alice and Ollie had spent the night in the cave, as they often did, and they had made all their preparations as secretly as possible the day before. Emily had a feeling that Mum and Dad were a bit suspicious, but since the arrival of Alice and Ollie they had been allowed further afield without their parents, so she hoped that they could get there and back without causing too much trouble.

It was a clear bright morning, and the sun was just rising as they tiptoed out and soared into the sky. Flying high, they could see a good distance ahead and Emily hoped she would be able to find the way. She and Tom both remembered the long stretch of

moorland between Ben McIlwhinnie's mountain and their old cave. They would have to land for a rest in the middle somewhere, and then look for landmarks to their old valley. As long as they didn't choose a marshy patch, they should be all right, Emily thought.

None of them had any breath to spare for talking as they flew on and on into the rising sun.

Some time later she became aware that Tom was lagging behind. He was the smallest of the four, and she had secretly wished that he would agree to stay behind, but there was no chance of that. Tom was quite determined to keep up with Ollie in everything.

Alice glided up close beside her. "We need to find a place to stop," she whispered. Ollie rose a little and hovered, scanning the ground below.

"There's a place!" he called down to them, pointing ahead. "See those rocks? We should be safe down there."

He led them on a gentle glide towards a stony patch of ground on the moor, with big boulders lying around. As they landed, Emily realised that the place looked familiar. "Tom!" she said. "This is the place where we had our picnic in the rain, isn't it? When we were on our cave hunt in the spring?" Tom nodded, but was too out of breath to say anything.

"If you're sure, that proves we're on the right track," said Ollie, pleased. They settled down for a welcome rest and a drink, and Tom slowly recovered and began to look more like his usual perky self.

"Come with me to the top of these rocks," said Ollie to Emily after they had finished their snack. "See if you can spot any landmarks to help us find the cave." The two of them flew higher and Emily peered into the distance.

"I think the shape of that mountain at the edge of the moor looks familiar," she said. "If we aim for that I should be able to recognise our glen."

"It's still a long way off," said Ollie quietly. "I don't think Tom's going to make it, do you? Not if we want to get back home tonight. We're having to fly fast, that's the trouble."

"I know," said Emily, worried. "I wish we hadn't brought him, but he'd have made such a fuss if we'd left him behind. What shall we do?"

"Leave it to me," said Ollie, and the two of them flew back to join the others.

"Right," he said briskly as they landed. "Change of plan. And no arguing! Allie, you and Tom stay here with the bags. Make a camp – do a bit of foraging, gather some beetles and things to take home. Emily and I will fly on, find the cave and then come and report back. Then we can all fly home before it gets dark and the parents start to get in a flap. OK?"

Alice looked at him and then at Emily. She realised why the plan had been changed, and understood what Ollie was asking her to do. As Tom opened his mouth to argue, she broke in. "Good idea. I'm feeling a bit tired to be honest. Will you be able to find us again on the way back?"

"No problem," said Ollie. "We'll send a Huff as soon as we get there, and you can send a message back. Good thing you and Emily are so good at reading Huff." Dragons can send quite complicated messages with smoke signals, and the four of them had been practising their signalling over the summer. Emily and Alice had got very good at it and often sent messages between the cave and the camp in the evening.

15

"It's not fair!" Tom began, but got no further. Ollie buffeted him round the ear with one wing, told him sternly to do as Alice told him and not wander off, and prepared to fly on with Emily.

"We'll be back as soon as we can," said Emily to Alice, and then they were off. Alice and Tom waved as they sped away.

"Right," said Alice, firmly, before Tom could start to argue again. "Let's see who can collect the most snails."

Ollie and Emily flew steadily without speaking, aiming for the distant mountain slope. As they left the moor behind, Emily started to recognise the land beneath them, and soon she spotted the river that ran through their glen. "Left a bit," she panted to Ollie, "we mustn't go too far down the valley. Follow that stream. Better keep a lookout for Humans too, in case they've started to move up the glen."

Ollie followed her directions, secretly hoping that they might see some. He had always enjoyed trying to stalk stray Humans when they lived in the south, and had once hidden and terrified a group of youngsters with a good fiery huff, before he was found and grounded by his father.

Emily now knew the way, and led Ollie confidently up the slope to the flat ledge where their old fireplace had been. The two dragons landed safely and stretched their tired wings.

"Well done," said Ollie, "brilliant navigating! Not a bad place, but not as good as the cave you've got now."

Emily looked around. She had expected the grass would have grown over the summer and covered their old fireplace, but to her surprise she saw a charred patch, and some half-burnt gorse branches lying around.

"Something's been here since we left," she whispered. "It can't have been another dragon, can it?"

"I don't think so," said Ollie grimly. He pointed to the cave mouth and Emily saw three brightly coloured cans lying crushed and empty amid a scattering of silver paper. "Looks more like Humans to me. Let's look inside, but go carefully and be ready to fly up if I say."

Emily held her breath and followed him into the old familiar cave. Her parents had cleared it very carefully in the spring, leaving no traces of the years they had lived there. But again there was strange rubbish lying around – empty bags that crackled and smelt peculiar, and more paper. Emily picked up a piece of pink elastic with two bright shiny bobbles at each end. She had no idea what it was, but she decided to take it to show Alice.

"Nothing here now," whispered Ollie, "but Humans have definitely found the place, so there's no way we can come and live in this cave. What a waste of a flight!"

Emily felt like crying. She had really thought this might be a way of keeping Alice and her family near enough to keep in touch over the winter, and it had all come to nothing. "I'm sorry!" she said, trying to keep a sob out of her voice.

Ollie looked surprised. "Not your fault!" he said. "It was a good idea. We'll just have to look a bit further afield, that's all. Let's send a quick Huff to Allie to say we're on our way and get back. It's a long way home." He sent a few puffs into the sky before spreading his wings.

Sadly, Emily took a last look round her old home before she took off from the ledge and followed Ollie. She kept her eyes fixed ahead, looking for Alice's answering Huff and didn't look back.

Neither of them spotted a solitary Human, dressed in a brown jacket and an old woolly hat, lying flat in the heather further down the glen. He was staring at them through binoculars with an expression of amazement on his face.

Chapter 3

Four In Disgrace

Alice had huffed, ***be as quick as you can***, so Emily and Ollie set a straight course for the puffs of white smoke she sent up at intervals to guide them back. But even though they had flown as fast as they could, the sun was sinking when they reached the rocks and saw Tom and Alice waving a welcome. They glided down, both feeling weary, and not in the least looking forward to the journey home.

"We found lots of snails," said Alice as soon as they landed. "Have some, and here's a drink. We need to be off as soon as we can."

"Did you find our cave? Are you going to live there? Did you see any Humans?" Tom, quite recovered from his weariness, danced up and down with excitement.

Ollie shook his head. "No good," he said between gulps of water. "Humans've been there. Found the junk they left behind."

"Were you seen?" Alice asked in horror.

"No," said Emily. "But the cave is no use if they know it's there. And I'm so tired! I'll never manage the flight home."

"But we must go!" said Alice in dismay. "They'll be so worried if we don't get home before dark."

"You're right," said Ollie, crunching the last of his snails. "I'm tired too, but we have to try. Come on, Emily, you can do it. Have another drink and finish your snails. We'll fly lower and take more rests if you need them."

Emily heaved a deep sigh and got up wearily. "Don't leave me behind then," she said as they took off.

This time Alice and Tom took the lead, flying straight towards a stand of pine trees far away at the edge of the moor. They had flown over them that morning, so they knew that was the quickest way home. From there they would be able to see the strange shape of Ben McIlwhinnie in the distance, and know they were nearly home. But it took them a long time, and Emily was almost falling out of the sky with weariness long before they reached the trees. Ollie, flying just in front of her, wasn't complaining, but she had a feeling he was tiring too. The sun had set into an orange glow behind the hills, and the sky was changing slowly to a deeper blue, striped with pink sunset clouds.

Alice looked back and realised how far behind they were. Calling to Tom, she led the way to the ground, landing on a small hillock. Emily landed in a heap beside her, breathing hard. "I can't go any further," she panted, putting her head on the ground and shutting her eyes. She could hear Alice and Ollie talking above her, but was too exhausted to join in.

"We're not going to get home before dark. I think we'd better stay here tonight." That was Ollie.

"The parents will be frantic! Why don't I fly on and leave you three here. I could make it – I had a long rest, remember."

"You can't fly alone in the dark."

"I could go with Alice. I'm not a bit tired." That was Tom. Emily opened her eyes to protest, but before she could speak, Alice said, "No, Tom. You'd slow me down."

"We'll all have to stay. Much safer than trying to go on in the dark. I'm sure Dad would agree if he was here."

"I don't know…" Alice was still sounding very unhappy at the thought.

Suddenly there was an excited shout from Tom. "Look everyone. A HUFF!!"

He was right. Rising above the still-distant pine trees, but much nearer than the mountain, was a white smoke signal, clear against the deepening blue of the sky.

where are you

"Quick, all together!" said Ollie and the four of them put their heads together and huffed as hard as they could.

HERE

As soon as their huff was sent, Alice launched herself into the air until she was high enough to see beyond the pines. They could see her waving wildly, and in a short while the dark red shape of her father could be seen, flying fast towards them. They met in mid air and came circling down to land beside them.

It was obvious that Oliver was furious.

"Anyone hurt? Just tired? I suppose you realise we've all been out searching for you since sunset? I must let the others know."

He huffed his message into the sky, and Emily read – *found all safe lifts needed*. Then Oliver looked sternly round the four of them.

"How DARE you go off without telling us where you were going? We woke up to find you gone, and we had no idea where! So when it began to get dark, three of us had to fly in different directions to search. You should have more sense. Ollie, you're old enough to know better. I'm ashamed of you!"

Emily began to cry. "It was my fault!" she wailed. "It was all my idea!"

"We all agreed," said Alice. "We're all to blame. Sorry, Dad!"

"We were only trying to help you find a home for the winter!" Tom sounded defensive.

Oliver stared at him. "What? No, don't tell me now. Save it for later. We need to get you home."

He flew into the air and they saw him turn slowly, signalling. A few minutes later Duncan appeared, followed by Ellen. All three came to land on the hill. Alice rushed to hug her mum. "I'm sorry!" she sobbed. "I'm so pleased to see you!"

Duncan looked at Emily and Tom. "Are you all right? Then let's get you home. Ellen, can you take Tom if I carry Emily? What about the others? You can't manage two, Oliver!"

"Ollie can fly himself home!" Oliver was obviously still angry with his son, but Alice interrupted.

"No, Dad. Ollie's flown much further than me today. I can fly."

Ollie looked as if he might protest, but at a look from his father he climbed onto his back without a word. Emily and Tom climbed up too, and the three dragons, with their tired passengers, launched themselves into the air for the flight home, with Alice keeping close behind. Half way home, Alice and Ollie changed places, but by then Emily and Tom were almost asleep.

26

When their mountain came in sight their spirits rose. Emily and Tom were looking forward to telling their news to the grown-ups round the fire over a nice hot supper, but they were disappointed. Oliver signalled to his son to fly straight to their camp, and followed him, carrying Alice. They didn't even have time to say goodbye. Ellen took a minute to land and tumble Tom off her back before following them. Obviously they were all in deep disgrace. There was to be no welcoming feast for any of them!

Gwen was waiting outside the cave looking very relieved, though annoyed as well. Emily was just about to give her a hug and say how sorry she was, when Tom shouted, "Why couldn't Ollie have stayed for supper. We've got lots to tell you!"

There was a loud wail from inside the cave. Gwen stopped looking pleased to see them and frowned. "Oh, Tom, you've woken Lily! It took me ages to get her to sleep. She wanted Emily to read her a story. Duncan, give them a bite to eat. Then it's straight to bed for both of them. We'll talk about this in the morning."

She stomped into the cave as Lily's wails increased. Emily felt more and more guilty. "Can I read to Lily now?" she whispered.

"No," said Duncan, and gave them some cold supper without saying any more. Then he relented and made them some hot mint tea, which Emily was too miserable to enjoy. Tom was starting to mutter rebelliously, but Emily just wanted to go to bed and sleep. As they went inside, Tom whispered, "It's not fair! We were only trying to help! I need to talk to Ollie in the morning."

"Well, I hope you'll be allowed to," said Emily. "I have a feeling we might be grounded."

"They can't!" Tom exclaimed. But Emily knew they could. She climbed into her heather bed with aching wings and tears in her eyes. Everything had gone wrong!

Chapter 4

A Problem at the Camp

The next day was horrible. Gwen and Duncan were horrified when they learned that Emily had been all the way to the old cave, and when she told them of the Humans' litter inside they were even more annoyed.

"After all we've taught you about the dangers of Humans!" Duncan exclaimed. "How could you be so stupid, Emily? You and Ollie might have ended up in cages! None of us would be safe."

"And Tom, you know perfectly well you can't fly so far," Gwen added. "You knew it was a long way. You seem to think you're as strong as Ollie is, when he's a lot older than you."

Tom looked mutinous. "I keep telling you, we were only trying to help. It wasn't our fault that Humans had been in the old cave. If we had found it empty it would have been perfect for Ollie and the family all winter, and then you'd all have been pleased. It's not fair!"

"Don't be cheeky," his father said sternly.

"I think it would be better if you stopped seeing so much of Ollie. He's a bad influence."

"He isn't!" Tom muttered. Emily glared at him. She thought he was making the situation worse.

"I'm really, really sorry," she said. "It was my idea in the first place, and I knew it was a long way to go. But I thought we'd be all right, and I *did* think the cave might do for them. We all hate the thought that they're going away. Please, *please* can we all get together and talk about it? We want to know what they're going to do."

"You're not going anywhere today," said Duncan. "Take that scowl off your face, Tom, or you'll be grounded tomorrow as well. I'm going fishing – and no, you can't come!" He spread his wings and soared down to the loch where the Otter family lived.

Tom scowled even more when his mother, on her way inside, remarked, "Your room hasn't been cleaned and tidied since the Gramps left, Tom - so that's what you can do today."

"IT ISN'T FAIR!!" he shouted as soon as she disappeared, lashing his tail and sending a spurt of angry flame into the air.

Emily sighed. "Shut up, Tom, you're making them crosser than ever."

"Huh, Miss Goody-Goody," sneered Tom angrily. "All you can do is cry and say you're sorry. Well, I'm not! And I bet Ollie isn't either."

Without waiting for her to answer back, he stomped into the cave.

Emily spent most of the day looking after Lily, but she was too miserable to enjoy it, and Lily got bored and grumpy. Tom was still not speaking to her. By supper time, all Emily wanted was to go to bed with her favourite book. There had been no sign of the others at all, but while they were eating their supper, they saw a Huff signal rising above the wood in the distance.

problem here come tomorrow

"What can that mean?" said Gwen.

"I expect we'll find out tomorrow," said Duncan shortly.

Emily didn't dare to ask if she and Tom could go too. She saw Tom open his mouth and prodded him

31

sharply with her tail. Then she tiptoed into her own private cave to find her book, hoping things would be better in the morning.

Everyone was in a more cheerful mood after a good night's sleep, and Emily breathed a sigh of relief as she ate her breakfast. Afterwards, they all flew down to the camp, Duncan carrying Lily. Nobody had mentioned Tom and Emily staying behind, and fortunately Tom had calmed down and stopped making inflammatory remarks.

There was no sign of Ollie when they landed, but Alice was looking out for them, and managed to whisper to Tom and Emily, "The most awful thing has happened…"

"What?" they said together, but Alice had no chance to answer before her mother came up to them, with Georgie capering ahead of her, huffing excitedly. After that, there was such confusion of huffs and squeaks from Lily and Georgie, that Emily only had a chance to ask anxiously where Ollie was.

"He's…" Alice began, but got no further, as Ellen ushered them all into the middle of the camp where George was sitting by the fire. He was hunched up with drooping wings and looked tired and old. "Has Ellen told you?" he asked, looking up as they crowded around.

"No. What's happened?"

"We have a visitor!"

"Who?"

"My sister!" said a grim-faced Oliver, coming up with a load of wood for the fire. "She's called Angie. She arrived yesterday."

"What's wrong with her?" asked Tom tactlessly.

"You'll see. Shhh!" whispered Alice.

"And where's Ollie?"

"Shut up Tom!" said Emily. "I want to listen."

Old George was speaking. "…I think she is worried about me with winter coming on. She has a very kind heart really, Oliver. I know she can be difficult, but…"

"BUT WHERE'S OLLIE?!" Tom shouted. Emily sighed as she missed the last of George's words.

A voice came from above their heads. "If you mean my insolent nephew, he is in here. He will not

34

be coming out today. I have chained him up until he learns better manners."

Everyone turned and Tom and Emily gasped. Standing on the landing branch outside their tree-house was the most impressive dragon they had ever seen. She was apricot pink in colour with wings shaded in peach and pink and cream. Her talons were long and gleamed with gold. There were sparkling anklets round each leg and a huge necklace of bright emeralds around her neck. A small bag, which was also gold and sparkling with emeralds, dangled from one claw. She looked dazzling against the dark tree trunk.

As the dragon family below her stared up in speechless astonishment, she took a deep breath and blew three perfect smoke rings into the air. Then she spread her wings dramatically and looked down her long nose at the assembled company below.

"You must be the neighbours," she said haughtily. "Allow me to introduce myself. I am Lady Angelica. Sir George is my father, and I am here to rescue him. I consider *cave-dwellers* most unfit company for my father and his family."

Chapter 5

Aunt Angelica

Ellen broke the frosty silence. "Angelica, dear, why don't you come down and meet everyone properly? I've made some mint tea. We can sit by the fire and talk about this."

"Yes, do come down, Angie . . ."

"Angelica, Father! How many times do I have to tell you?"

"I'm sorry! Angelica. Do come and join us," said Old George, trying to ignore Oliver's ferocious scowl.

"Oh, very well!" Angelica spread her wings and glided gracefully to the ground. She landed with a clink of jewellery and smiled at them graciously, showing very white teeth. "I suppose you are natives of these parts. I have never met *blue* dragons before. Though you – Gwen isn't it? – are a most unusual shade of turquoise. Do you have Welsh blood by any chance?"

"My mother is Welsh," said Gwen, coldly.

"Ah, that accounts for it. And your daughter – hmm – quite attractive wings. I like the shading, dear. Rather more tasteful than Alice's spikes, I must say. Your boy is a pity, of course. Nothing one could do with such a vulgar shade of blue."

"I like it!" Tom muttered rebelliously. Angelica ignored him. Ellen handed round the mint tea and Alice followed with bramble biscuits, which Angelica refused haughtily though they were deliciously burnt and crunchy.

"Can I take one to Ollie?" she whispered to her mum. Ellen nodded, but unfortunately Angelica overheard.

"Certainly not!" she said. "No food until he apologises." Ellen mouthed 'later' as she sat down with her tea. There was an awkward silence round the fire. Gwen tried to be polite.

"Have you come far?" she asked.

"Many miles," answered Angelica. "I live far to the South."

"You surely didn't come alone!"

"Of course not! Naturally I brought my servant to carry my bags. I sent him back yesterday. He will look after my castle until we return."

"Castle!" Emily exclaimed. This was sounding more and more like one of her books!

"It's a ruin," said Oliver. "In the middle of a forest. Not nearly as grand as it sounds."

Angelica glared at him. "At least I have a roof over my head!" she snapped. "I'm not reduced to travelling the country and camping in the open air. And as for living in *caves* – well! It might be acceptable to Scottish dragons but it certainly isn't what *I'm* used to. The snow will be falling any day, and I cannot allow my father to live outside, in this dreadful climate, at his age. He must come south with me immediately. You will all come. There is plenty of room in the castle. Of course, the children will have to sleep in the cellar, but *my* cellars will seem *palatial* compared to this!" She swept a wing around the camp site, huffing with contempt.

"It's only the beginning of autumn," Duncan interrupted. "We won't have snow for weeks yet."

"Rubbish. Everyone knows it snows all year round in Scotland. This must have been an unusually mild summer."

"No use arguing with her," said Oliver to Duncan. "She never listens and she always knows best!"

George said nothing, but looked sadder than ever. Emily felt near to tears as she looked at him.

Suddenly Angelica gave a loud gasp and stood up, pointing across the fire. "Whatever is that?" she exclaimed. She was pointing straight at Lily, who had been scampering round and round a holly bush chasing Georgie, and was now coming to find her mother.

"That's our baby," said Emily proudly, fed up with Angelica's boasting. Lily lifted her wings to be picked up.

"A golden dragonlet!" Angelica breathed, almost to herself. She stretched out a claw to Lily who huffed back suspiciously, then giggled as Angelica clinked her bracelet. "May I hold her?"

"She doesn't know you…" Gwen began, but Lily climbed onto Angelica's claw and began to play with the beads. Emily started to protest, but then stopped herself. She had just noticed the bright blue shape of Tom creeping quietly towards the tree-house, clutching the last of the bramble biscuits. If they could distract Aunt Angelica for a little while, poor Ollie might get a welcome snack!

"She's called Lily," she said. "She hatched out of a *beautiful* egg in the spring. I was there when she hatched. I'm teaching her to talk. She loves playing with Georgie and she likes me to read to her…" She tried to keep talking, but Angelica was hardly listening.

"Beautiful!" she said, dangling her emerald necklace in front of Lily, who huffed in excitement and tried to grasp hold of it. "To think such a rare golden child should be found here in the wilds of the North."

Everyone was watching Lily but out of the corner of her eye Emily saw Tom reach the foot of the tree and start to climb out of sight. She grinned across at Alice who smiled back. She had seen Tom too, but would certainly not say anything! Duncan was looking furious at the insults to his family and his home, and Emily hoped he wouldn't explode before Tom got back.

Tom climbed the tree as silently as he could. As he reached the level of the tree-house he peered cautiously round the trunk and looked down. Everyone, including Aunt Angelica, seemed to be staring at Lily. Holding his breath, he slipped round to the door and climbed through the bracken fronds. Once he was safely out of sight, he heaved a sigh of relief and looked around.

Ollie was sitting at the far end looking furious and uncomfortable. A short length of golden chain fastened him to a branch by one leg, so he could hardly move and certainly couldn't escape. Tom pattered across the floor and produced the biscuit.

"What happened?" he asked.

"I hate that old…!" Ollie spluttered through a mouthful of crumbs.

"Yes, she's horrible," Tom agreed. "Can we get that chain off?"

"No, I've tried. It's too thick to melt with huff. I'll just have to wait 'til she lets me go."

"She says you have to apologise first."

"No chance! I called her a smelly old bat, and she is! She puts on *perfume!* Yuk! I don't know why she had to come."

"She wants you all to go and live in her castle. She said your Grandad *has* to go. Says he can't spend the winter up here. She thinks it snows all the time! She hasn't a clue."

"You can't argue with her. She never listens. If only that old cave of yours had been OK, Dad could have told her to shove off. He hates her too. We all do. Except Grandad, and even he gets fed up with her."

"What are you going to do?"

"I don't know," said Ollie. Tom looked at him in surprise. Ollie was the daring one, always full of ideas, but now he sounded as though he had given up.

"We'll think of something," he said. "Suppose I'd better get back. She's probably stopped gazing adoringly at Lily by now."

"What does she want with Lily?"

"Dunno. She was cooing over her. Really soppy. Then Emily started blethering, and I got the chance to creep away. I thought you might like a biscuit."

"You were right. I'm starving. I suppose I'll have to apologise if I want any supper. You push off now. Thanks, Tom."

Tom slipped out of the door and down the tree as quietly as he could. Anyone who could chain up his hero and threaten to starve him was a real enemy, he thought. Whatever were they going to do? As he reached the ground and wormed his way back to the fire he heard Angelica's haughty voice. "Where has that blue child gone?"

"I'm here," he said innocently, but fortunately Angelica wasn't really interested in him.

"Listen, everyone," she announced, still holding Lily on her knee, "I have decided what I shall do. If, as you assure me, there will be no snow in the next few days, I shall stay here for a short holiday. I cannot, of course, sleep on the ground, but I will make myself reasonably comfortable in there." She pointed to the tree-house. "I shall chain my nephew to a tree down here instead, until he apologises."

Oliver stood up, huffing ominously. "No you won't," he said. "You'll free him. Now! If you're going to stay here for a few days, you have to be a bit more reasonable."

"And we must be going," said Gwen firmly. "I'll take Lily now." She plucked the little dragon away from Angelica, who started to protest and then smiled sweetly.

"Do bring her to see me tomorrow!" she said. Gwen did not promise.

"Come on," said Duncan to Emily and Tom, and took off without saying goodbye. Emily waved a sad farewell to Alice before flying up. Alice was looking desperate!

"What a dreadful creature," said Duncan when they were on their way. "I don't envy them having her to stay!"

"And it's our tree-house she's stolen!" said Tom, huffing his fiercest flames in fury.

Chapter 6

Things Get Worse

Neither Tom nor Emily slept well that night. They were still suffering aching wings after their long flight, and they tossed and turned in their heather beds worrying about Alice and Ollie and how they would manage to convince Aunt Angelica that they did *not* want to live in her castle. Over breakfast they were both grumpy.

"Listen, you two – it really isn't our problem!" said Duncan. "We can spend the winter here, but we can't fit the others in as well. They have to decide what to do, and it isn't easy."

"They might decide to go with Angelica, you know," said Gwen. "It sounds as though they would fit into this castle of hers, even though it probably isn't nearly as grand as she pretends. Then they would be safe and warm all winter." She looked at the miserable faces of Tom and Emily and added sympathetically, "But I'm sure they'll come back up here in the spring. Ellen and Oliver like living by their loch just as much as the children do."

"Ollie will hate living with *her*," Tom muttered rebelliously.

"Ollie will have to put up with her!" Duncan said. "No use talking about it. Let them decide. Tom, come down to the loch with me. Those young otters want to see you. They say you haven't been swimming for days."

"Do you want to go too?" Gwen asked Emily, but she shook her head. When Tom and his dad had gone she sighed. "I wish Des was here. He'd know what to do."

Des, the wild and adventurous Traveller, had stayed with them for a while in the spring and helped them to find their friends. They hadn't heard from him since their exciting visit to the sea a few weeks earlier. He had promised to keep in touch when he left, heading south, but there had been no Huff from him for quite a while.

"We've no idea where he is," said Gwen. "You could try a Gloaming Huff, but I expect he's out of range. He'll be back sometime. But he can't help with this problem, Emily; it's for Ellen, George and Oliver to decide, as Dad says. Cheer up! They aren't leaving yet. What are you going to do today?"

"Can Alice come over?"

"Yes, if she's allowed to. Send a Huff and see." She went into the cave to see what Lily was up to.

Emily flew up to the top of their hill. It wasn't a hill at all of course; it was Ben McIlwhinnie, a sleeping mountain giant. Their cave was underneath his chair and their fireplace was between his boots; they often sat on the ledge of his knees where his huge hands rested and the top of his bald head was a splendid look-out point.

Emily sat up straight on his head, sent a Huff into the sky and sat down to watch for Alice's reply. It was a very still morning, with a hint of autumn mist across the lochs. She could hear the comforting sound of Ben's regular breathing, and remembered how frightened her family had been when he had first awakened and sneezed, whirling them all down the hill in a heap.

Now he was Emily's friend, and she was allowed to wake him up if she needed him. They had roused him to introduce all their new friends and to show him baby Lily, and he had stayed awake for three whole days after their welcome party. Sometimes during the summer he had woken up in the evening and told them stories, saying how much he enjoyed young company. She remembered the tales of times gone by that kept even Ollie spellbound, and how much Old George had enjoyed sharing memories with him. But now he had gone back to sleep, for the winter he said, and Emily knew that her parents wouldn't allow her to wake him again. This was a problem that they had to solve for themselves.

While she thought all this she was gazing down to the trees that hid Alice's camp, waiting for an answering Huff. Suddenly she spotted the distant puff of white smoke: *coming*. She huffed back *good* and waited until she saw the tiny shape of Alice rise above the trees heading towards her. She took off and flew to meet her.

They settled together on the ledge of Ben's knee and Alice told Emily a bit more about her glamorous aunt. "She's not as bad as Ollie thinks," she sighed as she finished. "She's quite kind really; it's just that she's bossy and always wants her own way, and Ollie's so cheeky he makes her mad. He wasn't allowed to come out today because he flew over her head and dropped two enormous spiders on it. She hates them. One ran down her neck and got tangled in her necklace. You probably heard her screams from here!"

"Is she really *Lady* Angelica?"

"Course not! She's called Angie! She just thinks Angelica sounds posh, and she added the Lady bit when she found her old castle. Now she calls Grandad 'Sir George' and pretends we're a very grand family. So Ollie calls her 'Auntie Anje' to make her mad, and stomps around being as rude as he can and encouraging Georgie to be naughty. Mum tries to keep the peace, Dad tries to keep his temper, and Grandad just looks sad. I was really glad to get away!"

"What are you going to do? Have they decided?"

"Not yet. But I have a horrible feeling they'll decide to go back with her, for Grandad's sake. We've nowhere else to go. I don't want to, and Ollie says he'll run away."

"You don't need to go yet! The weather won't get really cold for weeks."

"She doesn't believe that. She keeps saying it's going to snow."

"I wish Des was here," Emily said sadly. "I'm sure he'd think of something!"

Alice giggled. "Imagine her face if she saw Des! He's so scruffy and weird, with his rainbow spikes and his earring. And he couldn't really help, you know. He can hardly turn up carrying a cave for us to spend the winter in!"

"I think I'll try sending him a Huff all the same," said Emily.

A little later they flew down to join Tom at the loch. He was disappointed that Ollie wasn't with them, and threatened to fly over to the camp to see him. Alice persuaded him that it would make matters worse, and they went swimming with the otters instead.

Wattie and Lottie, the cubs they had met when they first arrived, were almost as big as their parents now. (Emily and Tom were surprised; dragons grow up much more slowly.) They were as wild as ever and much faster in the water than the dragons, even Tom who was a particularly good swimmer.

"Where's Ollie?" asked Wattie. "D'ye no' think he's big enough to gi's a ride? One a' a time, like?"

"You keep asking that, but he's not!" said Alice.

"Is he no' growin'?"

"Not fast enough."

"Ah wish Des'd come back!" said Lottie. "It's nae fun wi'oot him."

"We'd like him back too," said Emily. "I'm going to try a Huff this evening. But you two might be too big even for him to carry now."

After their swim the three dragons sat in a row on the bank while the young otters dived away back to their holt. "How do otters manage in the winter?" asked Alice. "Do they go south too?"

"No, they stay here," answered Tom. "They curl up in their holt to keep warm, and sleep a lot more.

There's always fish to be found somewhere, and the loch doesn't usually freeze right over. I expect they like playing on the snow and the ice too."

"It sounds fun!" said Alice. "Oh, I wish…" She heaved a deep smoky sigh and didn't finish, but the others knew what she meant.

Just then there was a flurry of wings and Ollie swooped over their heads and dived into the loch. He surfaced in a few minutes, blew hard and scrambled out. "Needed to cool off," he panted, settling beside them, and it was true – he was steaming faintly.

"I thought you weren't allowed out," said Emily in surprise.

"I'm not. I'm collecting wood. You haven't seen me. I had to get away from Awful Anje! She goes on and on – nag, nag, nag!"

"You just make her worse," said Alice.

"No he doesn't!" Tom defended his hero. "You *couldn't* make her any worse than she is already."

"The important thing is what the parents decide. Have they said anything today, Ollie?"

"Not to me. I keep overhearing them talking – arguing really. Dad doesn't want to go with Anje, but Mum is worried about Georgie as well as Grandad. I think she'll agree to go to this wretched castle for the winter, and I bet Dad comes round to it. What are *we* going to do, Allie?"

"What *can* we do? We'll have to go with them."

"Not me! There's no way I'm spending the winter being bossed around by that old bat! All that clanking jewellery and smelly perfume and fuss about manners. I can't stand it. I'm going to run away!" Tom cheered loudly. Alice and Emily smiled, thinking he was joking. But one look at the determined expression on his face made them wonder if he meant exactly what he said.

Chapter 7

Ollie Disappears

Tom tossed and turned in his bed that night, wondering what Ollie was going to do. He could hear the rustle of Emily's heather in the next cave, and knew she was restless too. There had been no response to her Gloaming Huff to Des. Ollie was reckless and daring – would he really run away? With part of his mind, Tom longed to go with him, but he was still a young dragon, and the thought of leaving his family and their lovely safe cave scared him more than he would ever admit to Ollie.

During the night it started to rain – heavy driving rain that soaked their fireplace and even found its way into the mouth of the cave despite the sheltering gorse bush at the entrance. Tom and Emily woke late and groaned when they saw the weather. The cloud was so thick that there was no chance of signalling to the camp, and flying would be most uncomfortable.

"Well, it's not snow, but it's certainly bad enough to prove Angelica right about Scottish weather," said Gwen. "I wonder if they're all right down there."

"They'll be fine! We've had rain on and off ever since they came."

Dad was right, Emily thought, gazing into the downpour. Dragon-hide is waterproof, so dragons don't make nearly so much fuss about rain as the Humans in her books. But she had a feeling that Angelica would prove more Human than Dragon when it came to rain, and the tree-house would certainly leak! She giggled at the thought of drips on Angelica's head, and watched as Tom and Lily clambered outside to splash happily in the puddles around Ben McIlwhinnie's boots. She finished the last of her breakfast and was wondering whether to join them when there was a shout from Tom on the far side of the gorse bush.

"Here's Oliver!" he yelled. There was a rush of wings and Oliver landed on Ben's right boot, huffing hard and scattering raindrops as he shook himself. Everyone came out to greet him. He looked worried.

"Have you got Ollie here?" he asked, before any of them could say a word.

"No," said Duncan. "Why? Have you lost him?"

"He's not at the camp. He must have left secretly in the night."

"Have you decided to go with Awful Anje?" Tom burst out, to his parents' horror.

Even though he was worried, Oliver had to smile. "Yes, we finally decided last night, after supper. Just for the winter. We'll come back. We really can't stay, not with my dad and Georgie," he added, almost apologetically, looking round at them all. "But why did you ask that, Tom? Has Ollie said something to you?"

But Tom had recovered and started to think more clearly. "No," he said, crossing his tail behind his back.

"Alice doesn't know where he is. I just hope he hasn't done something stupid. You know what he's like! I can understand that he doesn't want to go with Angie – neither do I – but we have no choice. You're sure you don't know where he is?" He looked closely at Tom and Emily as he said this, but they both shook their heads. "Well, if you *do* see him…"

"We'll send him straight home," Gwen nodded.

"Thanks. I'll keep looking."

"I'll come with you," said Duncan, spreading his wings. "We'll go and ask the otters." The two dragons soared down the valley until they were shadowy shapes in the grey sky.

Gwen looked hard at Tom and Emily, but they both looked innocent. "Well, I don't suppose he can be far away," she said, going out to check on Lily. Emily and Tom made a dash for the back of the cave to talk in secret.

"He's run away like he said," said Emily. "He could be anywhere. He didn't give *you* any clues as to where he might go, I suppose?"

"No." Tom sounded unusually subdued. "I just know he'd do *anything* rather than spend the winter with old Anje. You don't suppose he's managed to contact Des, do you?"

"I shouldn't think so. He's not very good at reading Huff. I wonder if he told Alice where he was going."

"He wouldn't. Old Anje might chain *her* up and torture her. Force her to tell!"

"Honestly, Tom, you do exaggerate! Let's be sensible. Where could he have gone?"

They were both quiet, thinking hard, when there was a sound from the cave entrance and Alice came in, dripping and out of breath. Emily welcomed her with a beaming smile and took them both into her private cave, where Alice could dry herself off on the heather.

"No sign of him?" Emily asked anxiously.

Alice shook her head. "Dad's still out looking, but we don't know where to start. He's such an idiot – he could have gone for miles if he set off as soon as we were all asleep." She was starting to look tearful. Emily knew that she was really very fond of her reckless brother, even though they always disagreed about taking risks with Humans.

Tom was slightly embarrassed, and rushed in with some suggestions. "I bet he's looking for a good hiding place. He might have gone to our old cave. Ollie would enjoy huffing any Humans away. He wouldn't be scared of them. Or what about that cave on the beach where we went with Des? He could hide in there easily..."

Alice shook her head. "That one would be no use. It's too shallow, and the sea would come right up there in a storm. And I bet the Dads think of your old cave and go to check. It's too obvious."

"Your Dad said you'd decided to go with Angie for the winter," said Emily despondently.

"Yes," said Alice sadly. "And they're planning to go back with her, so it could be soon. Perhaps Ollie's just gone somewhere close to hide and delay things."

"I bet she hates this rain," Tom put in. "Perhaps she'll go tomorrow and leave you to follow later. You could pretend to be ill so you can't travel. Then perhaps you won't have to go at all. Then Ollie will come back and you can stay all winter." He beamed happily, obviously thinking he had found the solution to all their problems, but both Alice and Emily were more realistic and shook their heads.

Emily sighed heavily. "If only Des was here!" she said. "I bet he would know what to do. I've tried

Huffing but he never replies. You don't suppose Ollie's gone to find him, do you?"

Alice cheered up a little. "That's an idea! Ollie had a big row with Dad because he wouldn't let him go off with Des. He's desperate to go travelling and he thinks Des is really cool. And that was *before* Aunt Angie arrived. He'll be even keener now! Des headed south-east, I think. He said he'd had enough of the north for a while. I think Ice Land was too much even for him! Ollie did have a long private talk with him before he left, and he wouldn't let me listen."

"Let's head in that direction and look for them," Tom said eagerly.

"No, we can't. But we could suggest it to the Dads when they get back. They may have found him by now – you never know. Let's see if it's still raining."

It was, and it didn't look as if it would ever stop! It was going to be a long day, Emily thought gazing down the misty valley, completely empty of returning dragons. Obviously Ollie had not been found.

Chapter 8

More Bad News

The three children had exhausted every possible indoor game and finally gone out in the rain to splash in the swollen stream when they spotted Oliver flying wearily back. He was alone. Gwen gave him some nettle tea to warm him up and they listened as he told of his fruitless search for Ollie.

"Duncan flew off to your old cave to see if he's hiding there," he finished. "He said he'd get back as soon as he could and meet at the camp. He hasn't sent a Huff, I suppose?" Gwen shook her head.

"I doubt if we could see one in this weather. It would be so much easier searching if we had a clear day! Why don't we come down to your camp to wait for him? You never know, he might be bringing Ollie with him. If not, we can all decide what to do next."

"Good idea. As long as you can stand another dose of Angie! She's always thought Ollie was too wild and he's proving her right, so she's even worse than usual. Of course, Ellen might have strangled her by now..."

Oliver finished his tea while Gwen collected Lily and they all flew down to the camp. Ellen and George had spent a dispiriting day searching the thickets of gorse and bramble in the woods near the camp, in case Ollie had found a good place and was hiding just to tease his family and anger Angelica. They were delighted to see everybody, though disappointed to hear that nobody had found any trace of the runaway. George was exhausted and Emily thought she had never seen him looking so old and grey. She sat down beside him.

"Where's Anje – I mean Angelica?" she asked.

"She's packing in the tree-house," Ellen said. "She's determined we should all start off to the castle tomorrow, but how can we leave without Ollie?" She sounded close to tears, and Alice gave her a hug.

"I'm sure we'll find him," she said. "Perhaps he'll come back when she's gone away. We can stay and wait for him."

"I'll be travelling with Angie," said George, and smiled tiredly as both Alice and Emily gave a wail of protest. "I must. I think she's right. I'm too old to spend the winter in the open. Without me you might manage here."

Just then there was a call from above. "Ellen… ELLEN!" and Angelica appeared on the landing branch. She looked down at the assembled dragons. "Oh Alice, you're back. You'll do. I need a little help. You can bring that *sweet* golden baby with you, if you like. She must be *so* cold out there in the rain." Without waiting for a response she disappeared back inside. Alice looked mutinous.

Ellen sighed. "Will you go and see what she wants, Allie? Please? I don't think I can stand any more of her today! She's been SO objectionable about Ollie."

"All right, I'll go. Shall I take Lily with me?"

"No," said Gwen firmly. "She's fine where she is." Lily was looking sleepy, and had tucked herself under

Emily's wing. Alice left reluctantly and Ellen sat down, anxious to hear about Oliver's fruitless search for their missing son.

"No point doing any more until Duncan gets back," he finished. "I'm sure he's nowhere around here, but the otters will keep an ear out overnight just in case he *is* close and goes down for a drink at the loch. If he hasn't been found in your old cave we'll need to go further afield tomorrow."

At that moment Alice reappeared. "She was very disappointed not to see Lily. She wants me to take up some mint tea," she said.

"Can't she fetch it herself?" Tom said indignantly.

"No, I'd rather she kept out of the way," said Ellen. "We can do without her when we're planning what to do about Ollie." She got up to fetch the tea.

"Would she like Georgie instead of Lily?" Tom called after her, and everybody laughed. For the last five minutes, Georgie had been trying to get Tom to play with him and was now pulling the end of his spiky tail with grim determination. Tom got up. "OK, OK, I'm coming! Don't make any plans for tomorrow without

me," he added, sounding quite grown-up all of a sudden, and pretended to chase Georgie down to the loch.

Ellen sighed with relief. "That was nice of him," she said to Gwen. "Georgie's been a real pest today!" She flew up the landing branch with Angelica's tea.

Emily nudged Alice, who nodded and leaned forward. "Dad, we've been thinking. Do you think Ollie might have gone away to join Des?"

"Have you heard from Des?"

"No, not a single Huff since he went away," Emily admitted.

"Pity he's not here. He'd be useful."

"But we know he was heading south-east," Alice continued, "and Ollie was really keen to go with him, remember? They talked in secret before Des left. He might have planned a meeting place, or just headed in that direction in the hope of finding him when he gets in Huff range."

Old George sat up at this. "That's the direction we head to Angie's castle. If I leave with her tomorrow, at least I can keep a sharp look-out and Huff you any news."

"That would be a real help." Oliver understood that George hated leaving them while Ollie was still missing, and was keen to feel he was helping in the search.

Ellen returned looking exasperated. "She's changed her mind *again*! She's decided to stay another day. She *says* it's because we've exhausted George today searching for Ollie. At least she's staying up there."

"I hope the roof's dripping on her head," Emily muttered to Alice, who chuckled and whispered, "Yes it is, but there's one dry corner and she's sitting in that painting her talons."

"It's getting dark," said Gwen, looking worried. "I hope Duncan's all right. It's time I got the children home, but I don't want to leave until he gets back."

"We can't go, Mum. We're fine. Lily's asleep and Tom and I can stay up late. I couldn't possibly get to sleep…"

She was interrupted by Tom, who came running back from the loch, followed by a protesting Georgie. "I think I spotted Dad coming back," he panted. "Listen!"

They all looked up, and in a moment the steady beat of wings could be heard and the dark blue shape of Duncan appeared over the trees. He glided down to earth, landed heavily and stretched his tired wings. He was alone. They waited until he got his breath back, then Oliver said, "Well?"

"I haven't found him. And I hope he never went near the place, because it's far too dangerous now. I saw quite a number of Humans there and they seemed to be searching for something. I hid and waited until they'd gone further up the glen, then risked a quick look in the cave. No sign of him. Lots of Human litter and I found this." He held out a crumpled piece of paper. "Emily, can you read it? It might give us a clue about why the place is full of Humans. Whatever it says, one thing's for sure. Life's getting far more dangerous. We HAVE to find Ollie before he puts us all at risk."

Alice and Emily smoothed out the paper and bent over to read it in the firelight:

LOCAL GLEN RIVALS LOCH NESS

Monster-hunters were out in force in the upper glen yesterd
after local twitcher Hamish Mackie reported sighting two
unusual flying creatures. "I was out with my binoculars
when I caught a glimpse of them," he said. "One was re
the other was blue, I think, but I couldn't see it so clearl
They looked like the pictures of dragons in my wee gr
favourite story book, but obviously that's imp
By the time I'd got my camera focu

Alice turned the paper over, but there was only a torn picture of a row of smiling Humans on the other side. For some reason they were all holding large vegetables! "That's all there is," she said.

Emily looked horrified. "Oh Dad, that must have been me and Ollie! We didn't see any Humans, honestly. But we did find things they'd left. That's why we knew the cave was no good to us any more."

"Well you were obviously spotted!" said Duncan grimly. "Just what we've always been afraid of. I knew that glen would soon be found. Thank goodness we moved when we did."

"At least there's no news of any dragon being captured," said Gwen, trying to be positive.

"Not here, anyway," said Oliver, taking the piece of paper from Alice. "But we don't KNOW they haven't found Ollie. They sighted the children several days ago. We daren't risk going anywhere near them to find out more."

"If he's been found and caged up we'll have to go and rescue him!" said Ellen. "I'm not having my son imprisoned in one of their zoo places." She sounded unusually fierce and looking at her, and the other worried grown-ups, Emily realised that the problem she and the others had caused was going to be very difficult to solve.

Chapter 9

Angelica Tries to Help

There was a silence round the fire. Emily saw tears rolling down Alice's face and even Tom looked subdued. Ellen was so angry that small spurts of flame were bursting from her nostrils.

Oliver put a wing round her. "It's dark. There isn't even a moon. We can't do anything more tonight. Let's have a quick supper and get to bed early. Tomorrow the weather might be clearer and we can decide what to do next. If we find Ollie's been captured, of *course* we'll go and rescue him. Duncan and Gwen will help, won't you?"

Everybody nodded, even the children, and Ellen tried to smile and her huffs faded a little. But not for long; a jingle of jewellery heralded the arrival of Angelica in their midst.

"Surely the supper should be ready by now. And it's time those children were in bed," she announced.

"Angelica... please..." Old George began hastily, but he was too late!

Ellen took a deep breath, and the jet of flame she produced made everyone jump. She advanced on Angelica furiously. "All this is YOUR fault! YOU drove my Ollie away, with your nagging and preening and chaining him up and trying to starve him. I felt like running away myself! I don't blame him at all. Take your fancy bags and go! Now! Get back to your wonderful castle, but don't think I'm coming with you, because I'm not. I'm staying here, with my friends, to wait for Ollie to come back. And if he doesn't, I'll go and find him myself!"

Angelica, open-mouthed, was backing away as Ellen advanced. The others stared in amazement, and Emily heard Tom give a subdued cheer. It really looked as though Ellen would attack Angelica with flames and claws. Angelica burst into loud terrified sobs as she backed into a bramble bush, covering her face with her wings. It was Old George who came to the rescue. He stood up tall, looking suddenly much more vigorous and commanding.

"Ellen, stop! Angie, come and sit down! I'm ashamed of the way you have behaved since you arrived. I have said I will come to your castle for the winter, and I intend to do so, because life will be easier for Ellen and Oliver if I go. Then it is up to them what they decide to do. But while you remain here, you will stop treating other people like your servants, and you will apologise for the trouble you have caused."

Ellen swung round and headed for her stores of food, the tip of her spiked tail catching Angelica a final blow as she left. Emily was sure it had not been accidental! Angelica's sobs increased, as Oliver shouldered past her on his way to help Ellen.

Duncan got up. "I think we should go," he said, uncomfortably and his family agreed, except Tom. "I want to hear her say she's sorry!" he declared glaring at Angelica.

George took charge again. "We would like you to stay," he said. "We have a lot to discuss if you're willing to help us."

"I agree," said Oliver, coming back with a steaming bowl and some mugs. "Ellen's bringing some food."

Duncan glanced at his wife, who nodded. "OK. I'll build up the fire, then we can make some plans," he said. They all huddled close together as the fire burned brighter and the food was passed round. Angelica was still sobbing quietly, but Tom noticed that she didn't refuse food, or a large mug of mint and nettle tea!

George broke the sudden awkward silence. "Angie…?" he prompted.

Angelica gave a final pathetic sniff. "All right, I am sorry if I drove Ollie away. But really I was only trying to help…" There was a derisive snort from Oliver. "I WAS!" she insisted. "I couldn't BEAR the thought of Father and DEAR little Georgie living outside in the freezing winter weather. PLEASE come and stay. There's room for all of you," she added, looking round the circle. "You CAN'T risk that lovely golden baby in the snow. I could look after her for you…" She faltered to a stop, looking pleadingly round the solemn faces. "Please let me help!" she finished, and dabbed at her eyes pathetically.

"We don't want..." Tom began indignantly, but his mother nudged him sharply. "Be quiet, Tom. My family is well prepared for winter," she told Angelica, firmly. "And Lily will be quite safe, thank you. The urgent thing is deciding what to do about Ollie."

Oliver leaned forward, ignoring his sister. "Alice, you suggested that Ollie might have headed south to find Des. Now that we know he isn't hiding in your old cave, I think we should try that next. I would like to get in touch with Des anyway. He'd be useful. What do you think, Duncan?"

"It's possible. I don't think Ollie would have just flown off without an idea where he was heading. I'll come with you tomorrow, if you like."

"But what if he's been captured? We must find out!" Ellen insisted.

"I don't see how we can!"

"Dad..." Emily ventured, "remember how we went down our old valley to find out about the Humans in the spring? We read what they were planning on that wooden board. And now we've read about the sighting on that bit of paper. Can't we go down to a Human place at night and see if we can find some more writing?"

"Last time we nearly got caught when that light went on," her father reminded her.

"It's a good idea, though," said Alice. "If Ollie HAS been captured, they're bound to write about it because it will prove dragons are not just in fairy stories. Me and Emily could fly with you and help you to read anything we find," she added hopefully. "Then there'll be four of us to rescue Ollie."

The grown-ups looked at each other thoughtfully, ignoring Tom's indignant snort.

"It's risky for the girls, but I suppose we might need them."

"I can read too!" Gwen pointed out.

"But we can't take Lily with us. Or leave her with Emily and Tom."

George spoke again with authority in his voice. "It seems to me we can do all of this together if we plan carefully," he said. "I still intend to leave with

Angie, but our direction is the same as the route Des took. If the four of us set out together, taking the girls and travelling at night, we will hopefully find a place where Des might pick up a signal. If we pass over a Human settlement, we can see if we can find news of Ollie. We might even glimpse a Huff from him. Ellen and Gwen must stay in case Ollie decides to return. We'll keep in Huff range and they can let us know if he comes back. Then you can return and I will travel on with Angie."

"But I can't fly in the dark!" Angelica wailed.

"You'll have to!" Oliver replied. "Tomorrow morning we'll send up a Huff to tell Ollie you're leaving. That might bring him back if he's still hiding close by." It was obvious that it would take more than one apology for him to forgive his sister.

Duncan stood up. "Time for us to go," he told his family. "We'll send the Huff from Ben's head tomorrow morning, and get ourselves prepared for the journey. Then we can leave at nightfall."

Emily and Alice exchanged excited glances as Emily spread her wings, but they were both feeling sorry for Tom so they didn't exchange triumphant High Fours, though they both felt like it. Tom was trying very hard not to shed tears of fury and disappointment and said nothing as the four of them spread their wings and took off for the shelter of the cave, carrying Lily. The rain had finally stopped and stars were shining between the clouds.

"Let's hope it stays fine tomorrow night," Duncan said grimly, looking up at the sky as they landed on Ben's boots. Emily suddenly felt that their cave was the most safe and comforting place in the world. She was looking forward to her adventure, but hoped with all her heart that her home would still be there for her when she got back.

Chapter 10

Night Flight

Emily was relieved when the next day was over and she was ready to leave with her father. Tom had hardly said a word to her all day because he wasn't allowed to go. Duncan had pointed out that his mother needed his help and he must be grown-up about being left in charge, but it didn't stop him sulking. The realisation that Emily was being taken because she could read, while he had never bothered to learn, was a very sore point. Lily had woken up on the flight home and refused to go back to sleep, so was tired and stroppy all day, and her mother was obviously very worried. Emily had escaped up to Ben's head as often as she could during the day, to check for any answer to their morning Huff, but there had been no signal from either Ollie or Des.

Dusk was falling when Emily and her father waved goodbye to their family and the cave and flew down to the camp. Alice, Oliver and George were ready for them but Angelica was still fussing about her belongings in the tree-house. It was obvious that Oliver had had enough!

"Angie, we're ready! I'm not carrying any of your stuff, so carry it yourself or leave it. If you don't come NOW we're leaving you behind!"

"No, please, NO!" whispered Ellen, making them all smile. "Georgie and I are going to stay in your cave while you're away," she added to Emily. "We'll all keep each other company. If Ollie does come back, he's bound to try the cave if he finds the camp deserted. I've left him a message."

"We'll find him, Mum," said Alice, giving her a hug.

"He'd never let himself be captured," Emily agreed, and Ellen gave her a hug too.

"Be careful, both of you. I know you'll be sensible. Here's your aunt at last!"

Angelica landed with her usual jingle, carrying an assortment of bags and parcels. Despite Oliver's warning, George took two. Duncan and Oliver, who were both carrying essential supplies for the journey, pointedly refused. They gathered close to listen to Oliver's instructions.

"We fly close together; Duncan leads, George and Angie in line with the girls in the middle, I'll go last. Steady pace. Girls, as soon as you start to feel tired, tell us. We can either stop for a rest or give you a lift. We can't fly too high because we're looking for a cluster of human lights. That's where we might find information. Duncan is going to head for the bottom of their old glen, which is in the right direction. All set?"

They all nodded silently, except Angelica, who clinked. Oliver sighed in exasperation. "Angie, take off that stupid jewellery! How can you move silently if you need to? You'll get us discovered!" They all watched as she sulkily took off necklace and bracelets and stowed them in her handbag. Then they took off, one by one, and circled the campsite. Looking down as they left, Emily saw Ellen, looking tiny and waving, and spotted her message to Ollie. "IN CAVE" had been laid out in charred sticks near the fire. Alice chuckled. "Even Ollie should be able to read that!" she said to Emily as they followed Duncan and headed away.

They flew for a long time without speaking. A half moon shone fitfully between racing clouds ahead of them, and stars winked above. There were no human lights, but the moon lit up small lochs and streams between the trees. After quite a while, Emily saw something she recognised ahead of them. "Dad!" she said breathlessly.

Duncan turned his head. "Need a rest?"

"No, I'm fine, but isn't that the place with the yellow dragons down there?"

"The building site? Yes, I believe it is. There's the square hut and the fence we flew over."

"Can we land and see what we can find?" asked Oliver from behind them.

"No. A bright light comes on. Too dangerous. But it proves we're on the right track. This is the bottom of the glen, and I think if we go a bit further we might find the lights we're looking for. Alice, are you OK?"

"Yes."

"Good girl," said Old George next to her, sounding proud. There was a tremulous sniff from Angelica, but she was ignored.

Now they were following the bright line of the river as it flowed downhill. Emily was just beginning to feel that her wings were getting shaky when they all spotted a line of twinkling lights ahead, leading to a brighter cluster beside the river. The moon came out and they could see that a settlement of Humans lay below.

"Time for a bit of exploring," said Duncan, leading them downwards towards a thick belt of trees at the edge of the lights. They flew down in single file, dodging branches, and landed in a clearing, close beside a little stream that was hurrying towards the river below. They all had a welcome drink of icy water, Angelica shuddering theatrically, and a bramble biscuit each, and gathered close to discuss a plan of action.

"There're still a few hours of darkness. Do we press on or sneak into that human place to see if we can find any news of Ollie?"

"Oh do let's go on! I can't *wait* to get back to the castle." That was Angelica, but again she was ignored.

"I think we should have a quick look around here," said Oliver. "Why don't you take Emily into this... what do the Humans call it?"

"Village, I think," said Alice, and Emily nodded.

"See if you can find any more writing, Duncan, then come back and meet us here. Can you manage that, Emily? The rest of us can have a decent rest, and we'll go on if there's enough of the night left. I can give Emily a lift if she's tired."

"Right," said Duncan, spreading his wings. "Come on Emily." Emily tried not to feel too proud as she followed him. She hoped Alice would have a chance to explore at the next village.

They left the sheltering trees and then flew low and followed the line of lights into the village, keeping a cautious look-out all the way. The village seemed deserted and all the houses were dark and silent. Silently Duncan pointed to where brighter lights shone ahead and Emily nodded and followed him. They glided to land at the edge of a wide area with trees growing strangely out of the hard ground. Emily shuddered. It wasn't natural at all! A large black cat, crossing the square, froze and hissed at them, then fled between the houses and disappeared. Nothing else moved.

"Where on earth do we start?" whispered Duncan, sounding hopeless. Emily tried to remember all she had read about Humans and their villages. She pointed across the square.

"See that light over there?" she said. "I think that's called a shop. Why don't we go and see if there's any writing in the window. There's nobody about, so I think it's safe." They kept to the shadows as they crept across the square. When they reached the window, Emily climbed onto her father's back and stood up to peer over the sill. In the dim light she could see an array of bright plastic toys, a pile of woolly hats, some furry animals and to her excitement, picture books. "Dad!" she whispered. "There are dragons here! Stand up and look." She hopped down and allowed Duncan to stand and peer in. Duncan took a long look, then dropped down and crouched with Emily in the shadow of the building.

"I don't like it," he said. "It seems to me that Humans know too much about us. One of those pictures looked rather like Ollie – same colour. Do you think they've caught him?"

"No, that wasn't Ollie – even he doesn't look as fierce as that! Those were just books for children with pictures of dragons. It doesn't mean Humans believe in us, not really."

"None of this helps us find him. Let's go on a bit further."

They crawled cautiously along the edge of the street. They looked into one more lighted window, but it only contained slightly wizened vegetables and packets with writing on. Emily couldn't see anything useful in the writing so they carried on, passing silent and stationary machines in a variety of colours which gave a faint *ting* when you touched them with a claw. Duncan was just about to suggest that they call it a night and return to the others when Emily gave a horrified gasp and pointed across the street. Leaning against the opposite wall was an oblong board with large black letters:

Corrievechan Courier

GLEN MONSTER
MYSTERY
Experts Baffled
Exclusive Report

Chapter 11

Gloaming Huffs

Emily and Duncan flew back to the others as fast as they could, their hearts pounding. Emily felt quite confused, and was sure they were lost, but her father led her confidently to the exact spot where the others were resting. They were huddled together for warmth, as Oliver had decided it was too risky to light a fire. Alice was dozing but she woke up as they landed, and everyone listened eagerly to their news. When Emily recited the message from the board, Oliver gave a horrified gasp.

"They've captured him!" he exclaimed.

Old George tried to be reassuring. "It doesn't say that, exactly. It might mean he was seen and they don't know what he is. But they certainly haven't forgotten about us. Either they've got him, or they're still looking."

"We need to leave here as soon as we can!" Angelica exclaimed. "The sooner we reach the safety of my castle the better!"

Oliver huffed ominously. "I'm not leaving until we know for sure," he declared.

Duncan intervened. "Obviously we can't go anywhere until we find out more. But we shouldn't stay here; it's too close to this village place. Let's move away, back into the hills we flew over. We need to send a Huff back home as soon as it gets light, and we're still hoping to contact Des. Or Ollie, if he's still free."

Angelica sighed heavily, but everyone else agreed and collected their scattered bundles. "Climb on, Emily," Oliver insisted. "You've had no rest and you've done well tonight. We'll look for a safe hiding place and you can have a decent sleep during the day. Obviously we still need to travel at night." Emily agreed and climbed onto Oliver's back. Keeping close together as before, they headed for the hills.

The first streaks of dawn were visible in the east when they found a hillside so thickly covered with gorse bushes that it looked impossible for Humans to penetrate. It was difficult to find a place to stop, but flying low they found a small patch of bracken in the middle of the gorse, and landed to make a camp for the day. While George, Angelica and the girls tried to make themselves comfortable, Oliver and Duncan flew to the top of the hill to start signalling. Emily tried to stay awake until they came back with news, but she was too tired after her exciting night, and fell asleep almost immediately. Alice made George promise to wake her if there was any news, then burrowed into the bracken beside Emily and fell asleep too.

When they woke it was past noon, and bright sun was shining directly into their little camp. Oliver and Duncan were stretched out fast asleep, and Angelica was snoring rhythmically on the other side of the bracken clearing. They giggled quietly together as they listened to her. Then George appeared. He had been keeping watch from a rock sticking up out of the gorse not far away. He beckoned to them and they flew up to join him.

"Let them sleep," he said. "It's nice and warm here in the sun. Just be careful not to stick your heads up too high! We can't see that village from here, but that doesn't mean Humans aren't out looking for us."

"Did Dad manage to send a Huff this morning? Is there any news?" Alice asked anxiously.

"He sent a Huff to the cave, and they're all fine up there. Tom's being very helpful. Ollie hasn't come back, but there's been no sign of Humans near our lochs either, so that's encouraging. Everybody sends their love, and Ellen says it's lovely without Angie, but please don't tell her she said that!" The girls giggled and agreed.

"Can we send another Huff tonight?"

"Yes, we'll all come up here for the Gloaming Huff. Oliver said they *thought* there was a signal from the south, but it was too faint to be sure, so they'll try again tonight."

"Des!" said Emily and Alice in unison.

"No telling who it was. If it was a dragon at all…" He sounded tired, so the girls offered to stay on the rock and keep watch if he went down for another sleep, and he agreed gratefully and disappeared.

Emily and Alice lay in the sun, and Emily relayed as many details as she could remember of her visit to the village the night before. Alice was especially interested to hear about the books in the shop window. "I've seen those shop windows on our travels," she said, "but Dad's never allowed me to stop for a proper look. There are so many more Humans down in the south – you have to be on your guard all the time. Scotland is a much nicer place to live!"

"It sounds exciting though," said Emily. "Before you came, I found our old glen quite boring."

"It doesn't sound boring now!" said Alice.

"It's interesting seeing a bit more of Humans and their places, even if it is dangerous. Look at all those big metal towers in a line over there. Do you know what they are?"

"I've seen lots of them before we came up here. See the thin strings in a curve between the towers? Dad says they're called the Singing Strings, because they make a noise in the wind. You mustn't ever go anywhere near them, especially if you're flying. They could kill you, Dad says. It can be dangerous at night, but Dad and Mum always know when they're near, and keep us well away."

Emily thought again that Alice's life had been much more exciting than her own. She wondered if Dad knew about the Singing Strings. She looked at the long line of dangerous towers marching over the hills in the distance, and shuddered.

They kept watch for a long time while the grown-ups slept, but the only danger was from two large ravens who flew down to the rock to investigate, and peered suspiciously at them. Alice and Emily froze in horror, until Alice had the bright idea of scaring them off using a joint huff with a spurt of flame included. The ravens rose in the air and the girls heard one say, "Muckle tough lizards," and the other reply, "Did-nae look worth the peckin' onyways!" as they flapped away.

The sun was sinking and they were getting hungry when a stirring in the bracken below told them that the grown-ups were waking up. They flew down in time to hear Angie complain that her bracken was full of huge creepy-crawlies and she'd hardly slept a

wink. Trying not to snigger, the girls reported that they'd seen no sight of Humans all day. They all agreed that they needed some food before they flew up to the signalling hill, and though Angelica sighed loudly and muttered "Cold food again, I suppose!" they all felt better after a meal.

Afterwards they flew up the hill one at a time until they reached a rounded top, covered with sheep-nibbled grass and tiny wild flowers. They startled several sheep, which bounded away down the far side, but fortunately didn't make too much noise as they left. They heard the loud honk of a cock pheasant from below, then there was only the sighing of the wind and the song of a high skylark. But faintly, in the distance, they could all hear the ominous intermittent rumble of Human traffic from the road that led to the village.

"We're too close to them," Oliver muttered to Duncan. "The sooner we're back in the wilds the better! Are we too early to start signalling?"

"Try home first. They're probably keeping a look out."

Oliver and Duncan sent a steady stream of smoke into the still evening air, and they all gazed eagerly to the north until George told Angie, Emily and Alice to look in all directions in case there was a signal from anyone else. There was nothing to be seen, until George spotted an uncertain wavering column of smoke from the north. The Dads stopped Huffing and everyone turned and stared eagerly. The far-away signal stopped in a series of irregular gasps.

Emily suddenly realised what had happened. "I bet that's Tom!" she exclaimed. "He was on watch on Ben's head, but you know how hopeless he is at Huff!" For a minute she felt quite homesick.

"He'll have gone to fetch Gwen or Ellen," said Oliver, and they waited impatiently until a new confident series of Huffs could be read easily by everyone on the hill.

"No Ollie, but at least they're all safe back there," said George as Duncan and Oliver relayed their news back home. Alice and Emily sent a row of kisses, and Gwen Huffed that they would keep watch until darkness fell, in case there was any more news.

Oliver swung round. "Right, did you spot any-thing anywhere else?" Guiltily the girls confessed that they'd forgotten to look. "Angie?"

"I *think* I might have seen some smoke over there," she waved a claw vaguely, "but then it vanished. It didn't look like a proper message. I couldn't read it…"

Everyone stared into the darkening sky as Duncan sent up another signal. Emily found she was holding her breath. Then they all saw it.

hi des here whats up why are you down here

"DES!" shouted Alice and Emily together, danc-ing with excitement.

"SSSHH!" said Oliver, glancing round nervously. "Keep down. Anyone could be watching. We're on the skyline here!"

"Sorry – but it's Des!" Emily whispered.

"Sssh! Let's see what he has to say," George said quietly, and Emily and Alice calmed down. Duncan was still signalling.

looking for Ollie hes run away might have been caught by humans

ill come at once might have news can you stay where you are

100

bit close to humans well move down the hill a bit
ill find you should be there by dawn keep a lookout

The last signal ended with a row of dots, and Duncan swung round, beaming.

"You all saw that. He's on his way!"

Angelica huffed in irritation. "I suppose this means we can't travel any further tonight. I need a sleep in a proper bed, and a decent wash. Why does this Des person matter anyway?"

"Because he's brilliant!" Emily burst out. "He'll know just what to do."

"We wait for him here," Oliver decided. "I'll watch for a while. The rest of you go down the hill to that line of gorse. It'll give you some shelter. No, girls, you can't stay up. Get some sleep!"

"You'll need to be wide awake when Des comes," said Duncan as he led them all down the hill to find a place to sleep. They huddled together and settled down. Emily stayed awake for a long time, as the stars came out, quite sure she would never get to sleep, but eventually her eyes closed, and she didn't even wake when her father slid out to relieve Oliver of his watch on the hill.

Chapter 12

Des and the Helpful Hawks

I t was still dark when Emily woke up. Her father had gone, and she could not see Oliver either. The others were still fast asleep. She wriggled carefully from her place between Alice and Angie and stretched her wings, remembering the events of the previous evening. Had Des arrived? Not daring to fly, she scampered up the hill where she found Oliver and Duncan searching the sky intently. As she arrived at the top, rather out of breath, Oliver pointed a claw and looking south she saw a tiny orange flare. Duncan sent up an answering flame and they turned to see Emily.

"Is that Des?"

"Yes, we've been guiding him in with flares. He's not far away now."

"Shall I wake the others?"

"I think you already have!"

Looking back, Emily saw the dim shapes of George and Alice coming up the hill. There was no sign of Angelica. "He's nearly here!" she called as soon as Alice was near enough to hear, and pointed south.

It was George who spotted trouble. Everyone else was gazing eagerly towards the direction of Des's last Huff, but George looked down towards the village as he reached the top of the hill.

"I think we have a problem," he said quietly, pointing down.

A line of four small lights was moving steadily up through the gorse, following a narrow sheep path that they hadn't noticed before.

Oliver cursed. "Humans! They must have seen our signals. Perhaps even spotted us on the skyline. We've been careless. We need to go. No time to waste."

He turned to hustle them down the hill, but Duncan lingered to send a final message to Des. They heard faint shouts from the Humans below as they hurtled down the hill to rouse Angelica and leave.

Angelica was not pleased with her rough awakening, but several sharp tail prods from Oliver was enough to force her up. They grabbed their belongings and set off, flying low and fast away from the hill towards the direction of Des's last flare.

"I don't think they'll see us now," Duncan panted. "It's not light enough to spot us against the next hill. We can't risk flying high until we're further away. Can you keep up this pace?"

Everyone except Angelica agreed.

"How will we find Des now?" Emily gasped.

"I told him to stay where he was. I know the direction. We'll find him. But we need to put some miles between us and them before we signal again. And keep a good lookout. It'll be light soon."

They flew on steadily until the dangerous hillside was miles behind them. From time to time they had to skirt around Human buildings, but they saw no-one, and as it was getting light they found a thick pine wood and headed to the ground in its shelter. Even the Dads were out of breath. It was a cloudy morning, and much colder than the day before. Angelica shivered theatrically.

"Well, this is fine for hiding in, but no use for signalling to Des," said Duncan gloomily. He was just wondering whether it would be safe to light a fire when there was a flurry above them and a large sparrow-hawk landed on a low branch and gazed at them with her head on one side. She had fierce eyes and a large curved beak and the dragons looked up uncertainly. Angie gave a small scream.

"Saw you fly in here," the hawk said in a harsh voice. "Started circling and spying at dawn. Des asked me to find you. Stay here, I'll fetch him. Be a while."

She spread her wings and flew off through the trees. They looked at each other amazed.

"How does Des do it?" Oliver exclaimed. "Wonderful idea – getting a hawk to look for us! No Human will think there's anything odd about a sparrow-hawk flying around."

"Des gets on well with birds," said Alice. "Remember how he told us about the Bonxie who helped him in Ice Land?"

"Des'll find Ollie for us, I bet," Emily said. "He's brilliant!"

"So you keep saying," Angelica snapped. "While we wait around in the cold for this *brilliant* friend of yours, how about some breakfast? I suppose you won't risk a fire? I, for one, feel the need of something hot."

"Better not," said Oliver, "but I agree about breakfast." He fished in a bag and shared out dried slugs and oatcakes. Alice and Emily found a patch of brambles a little further into the wood and they collected a bag of large juicy berries, carefully saving some for Des. They noticed that Angelica, who didn't offer to help, had quietly opened her handbag and replaced some of her jewellery. "Is she getting ready to impress Des?" Alice whispered, and they sniggered at the thought. Old George had settled down for a snooze while they waited. Oliver and Duncan were foraging, but staying within call.

They heard the hawk before they saw her, and rushed back as she settled on the same branch as before. Two minutes later a familiar grubby green

dragon came weaving round the tree trunks and landed beside them. Emily and Alice rushed to give him a hug and the others gathered round.

"Great to see you all!" Des exclaimed, High Fouring Oliver and Duncan and clapping George on the shoulder with one wing. Then he sat down, putting wings round Emily and Alice. There was a meaningful cough from Angelica. "Please introduce me," she said coldly to Oliver, who muttered, "Sorry – Des this is my sister Angie."

"Angelica." She smiled sweetly.

"Hi," said Des, waving a casual claw but not moving from his seat between Alice and Emily. "OK, what's the trouble? Ollie's missing, you said in your Huff, but it wasn't very clear."

Angelica moved away a little and huffed haughty smoke rings into the trees with her nose in the air, while Oliver, ignoring her, told Des how Ollie had run away and why. Then Duncan took over, and explained how they had found out about the renewed Human interest in dragons. "So we still don't know whether Ollie's been captured," he finished. "We thought we'd go back tonight to see if we could find out more."

Des looked thoughtful. "Difficult. I haven't heard any rumours of a capture. You were lucky to find that bit of paper in the cave – and to have clever girls who could read it! OK. I think we need to try listening in to some Human conversation. I know, I know!" he added holding up a claw. "It's dangerous. But possible. Don't tell me you've never listened in to the Humans? It's always a laugh!"

Both Oliver and Duncan looked a bit sheepish. "Well… yes, obviously, once or twice, when I was *younger*," said Oliver, and Duncan added, "All right, yes, but you don't take risks when you've got a family, Des." George nodded solemnly, but with a twinkle in his eye.

"The three of us could try tonight," Des suggested, "but in the meantime we could get the hawks to help." He looked up into the tree but the sparrow-hawk had vanished. "No worries, she'll be back. Hawks fly far and wide and can see for miles when they're flying high. If we have a few of them, they could comb the country for Ollie. He's such a bright colour that he'll show up well from the air."

"Why should they bother to help us?" George asked.

"Are you friends with them, like the Bonxie?" Emily asked.

"Yeah, it's because we all met up at Safari Park! Remember we let some owls out of their cage before we left? After that little adventure with the lads and the elephants?"

"Of course I remember. They flew away in a line!" Emily remembered.

"Right! Well, it's not so far from Safari Park as the hawk flies, and word spread. The owls and hawks round here reckon they owe dragons the odd favour. It's been worth a few decent meals I can tell you! I'm sure Sukki can persuade a few friends and relations to recce for us."

"It's a brilliant idea!" Alice exclaimed. "Humans won't be suspicious of hawks!"

At that moment the hawk returned to her branch carrying a dead pigeon, which she proceeded to tear to pieces and devour. Angelica shuddered as feathers floated down, but Des called up, "Pigeon? Any chance of a couple more when you've finished?" The hawk nodded with her beak full.

"Pigeon's good eating! You don't get as many up in the wilds, but there are lots down here. Why don't we move a bit further into this wood, find a nice clearing and risk a wee fire? While our pigeons cook I'll see what Sukki thinks of my idea."

It did not take them long to fly through the trees and find a suitable clearing, and by the time they had settled and collected some sticks for a fire, Sukki had returned, with a second hawk, slightly smaller. They each carried a dead pigeon, which they dropped by the fire.

"Thanks – sure you can spare them?" Des said.

"Course! Harvest field over there full of them. So fat they can hardly waddle, let alone fly. Need any more?"

"Well…" Sukki nudged her companion who took off. She sat preening her feathers while Des outlined

the problem of the missing Ollie and the difficulty of dragons searching themselves.

"Aye, should be easy enough," she agreed. "Our three kids need flight and recce practice. A red dragon you say? I'll get 'em out the nest right now and set 'em off. Time they got up."

She left and George shook his head admiringly. "Wonderful!" he murmured, plucking the second pigeon. A few minutes later, Sukki's mate arrived with TWO pigeons in his talons and helped with the plucking. Then he flew away to join his family and organise the search.

Chapter 13

News at Last

E ven Angelica had to admit that roasted pigeon was delicious. When they finished Emily produced her secret horde of Des's favourite bumblebugs and gave him two. Angelica refused haughtily, but everyone else crunched loudly with enjoyment. They were feeling much more hopeful. Des seemed so confident that Ollie would be found.

When they had stamped the fire out safely, they filled in the waiting time by telling Des all about Angelica's castle, and the plan for Oliver's family to spend the winter there. To Emily's surprise, Des thought it a good idea. He questioned Angie about the castle, and finally got her to admit that it was actually a derelict house, largely ruined, situated in overgrown woodland and surrounded by a high wire fence to keep Humans from getting in.

"Sounds nearly as good as a cave!" he said finally. "I think you're right to take the family down there, Oliver. You need some shelter in the winter. I might even come and stay myself if the weather turns bad!" To Emily's surprise Angelica smiled graciously and said he would be welcome. She looked at Alice in astonishment. George winked at them, but said nothing.

"How far is it?" asked Des, and was told it was another night's travelling time. He looked thoughtful. Then he jumped to his feet. "Come on you two," he said to the girls. "Let's go foraging while we wait." He led them further into the wood, where they found more brambles, a bush of juicy rosehips and some colourful fungi which he assured them were really tasty. While they picked, they told him all that had happened since he left. He was impressed by the expedition to their old cave, and assured Emily that she and Ollie couldn't possibly have known there was a Human hidden in the glen, which made her feel a lot less guilty. She confessed that she and Tom were dreading a lonely winter without their friends.

"A winter isn't very long," Des said comfortingly. "We all sleep a lot more, and your cave will be cosy. I'm sure Alice will be back in the spring."

Before Emily could argue they heard a low call and hurried back to find five sparrow-hawks, three of them youngsters, perched in a row on a branch, and the dragons grouped below looking disappointed.

"No sign of him," Oliver said as they joined them.

"How far did you go?" Des asked the hawks.

"Fair stretch, far as the big river," Sukki said. "Sorry, kids need a roost now."

"Looks like we need to try your spying-on-Humans idea then," said Duncan reluctantly.

"Humans?" cried Sukki's mate suddenly, making them jump. "That Human cage-place, with they weird birds wi' hoods on! If yer boy's been caught, he might ha' bin taken there."

"Did you fly over it?" Sukki asked one of the youngsters, but the bird fluffed out his feathers and shuddered. "Naa, place gi'es me the creeps."

"I'll go see. Back to the nest you three, ye've flown enough for one day."

The dragons chorused their thanks as the young hawks left with their father, and they heard one say, "Can we go past the pigeon field first? Ah'm starvin'!" as they flew off.

"Is it like Safari Park?" Duncan asked Sukki.

"No' as bad as that! They live in wooden huts with wire cages on. Quite big ones, branches and things inside. There's a couple o' eagles, a buzzard and some other big birds, dunno the names. But they're taken out a lot, so they get to fly. Humans put daft wee feathery hoods on them so's they can't see and carry them off. Then they let them fly and hunt and call them back."

"Why don't they fly away? I would!"

"Dunno. They have danglin' things hangin' from their feet, so you c'n tell they're not free birds. They land back on the Human's hand and get taken back. I think they must've hatched in that cage place and don't know what it's like to be wild." She shuddered and her feathers fluffed so that she looked twice her normal size. Then she settled to preening.

The dragons looked at one another, baffled. "Well, we'll know soon," said Des. "Then we can decide what to do tonight. I need a snooze. Can't remember my last decent sleep!"

"You girls should rest too," said George. "It might be a busy night."

"If you go to spy on Humans, can we come too?" Alice asked hopefully.

"NO!" said their Dads, in chorus.

"Nice try!" said Des sympathetically as he closed his eyes.

They were all dozing when the hawk returned, even Sukki, asleep with her head under her wing. But they woke up hurriedly as he landed and proclaimed loudly, "They've got 'im!"

"WHAT!!"

"S'true. I saw him. Huddled at the back o' one of their cages, tryin' to hide."

"Is he hurt?" asked Oliver breathlessly.

"Seemed OK. Just scared. There was three humans lookin' in at him, so we couldnae talk. I perched in a tree and listened. Seems they're plannin' to send him off to some zoo. They were talking about special clothes so they wouldnae get burned. Sounds like your lad's done a bit o' fightin' back!"

"We have to get him out," Oliver said.

"Yes – tonight!" said Des. "Will you take us there?" he asked the hawks.

They looked doubtfully at each other. "We're no good flyin' in the dark," said Sukki. "Might find you an owl that knows the place, though. I'll send one over at dusk. I'd better get back to the nest now, check on the kids. Best of luck! You stay and help them plan," she added to her mate, and took off. The dragons called goodbye gratefully as she flew away.

"I wonder why Ollie hasn't tried to huff his way out," Duncan said.

"Probably can't produce enough flame," said Des. "It took four of us to melt a hole in the cage at Safari Park, remember. But there are five of us now, seven if you add the girls. I only hope it's the sort of wire you can burn away. We have to try. I vote we all go together as soon as the owl arrives."

"It might be dangerous," said Angelica doubtfully. "Do the girls and I need to go?"

"Of course we're going!" said Alice indignantly.

"We need to stick together, and then we can make a quick escape as soon as we've freed Ollie," Des said, to Emily's relief.

"Will there be Humans around at night?" George asked the hawk, who shrugged, "Dunno!"

"We go carefully, but if necessary we attack!" said Oliver fiercely. "We're getting Ollie out of there!"

Chapter 14

Rescue

E mily woke with a start some hours later to find a large tawny owl sitting on the branch talking quietly to Des and the Dads. It was very dark in the wood and she shivered. She nudged Alice awake and the two of them crept up to listen. Oliver turned to them.

"Wake George and Angie," he whispered. "We're going now, in case the clouds lift later. The darker the better." As soon as they were all assembled, Des whispered instructions to fly close and follow the owl and they took off, weaving between the trees until they reached the edge of the wood. The owl soared ahead to check for danger, but nothing was stirring. When she wheeled back, hooting, they flew up together and followed her, Des leading and Oliver bringing up the rear.

It was quite a long flight in the dark. They flew over the lights of a village, but when that was left behind, there were few signs of humans. Buildings were dark and they could hardly see the cows and sheep in the fields below. They crossed the shining expanse of a wide river, the dark bulk of a pine plantation, and then the owl hooted again and prepared to glide lower. They followed and landed in the shadow of a huge spreading sycamore tree in the middle of a field. The owl perched on the lowest branch while the dragons gathered on the ground, breathing heavily but trying not to huff. A number of cows were lying down further into the field, but they didn't get up, and they could just see the outline of buildings behind a hedge.

"Over there," the owl pointed a wing. "Sukki said your lad is in the end cage. You have to pass the eagles. Make sure they don't shriek or the dogs might wake."

"Could you fly over and check there are no Humans out?" asked Duncan.

"Will do!" She flew over the hedge and reappeared a few minutes later.

" No Humans, no dogs. What do you plan to do?"

"Go in – all of us together – melt the wire and get him out!" said Oliver fiercely.

The owl chuckled. "You were good at that!" she said, and Emily realised with surprise that she must have been one of the owls they had relcased from Safari Park in the spring. "I'm off for a spot of hunting," she added. "But I'll stay around in case you need me."

The dragons huddled together to make whispered plans. "We don't want to pass the other cages," said Duncan. "Let's head for the far end of that hedge and see if we can find a way through."

They crept through the grass as quietly as they could, wings folded tight. One of the cows lumbered to her feet and they froze, hoping that she wouldn't let out a warning bellow, but she just took a few suspicious steps towards them, then stood staring and breathing heavily. They carried on and soon they were all gathered in the shadow of the hedge. It was thick and impenetrable.

"No good," said Des. "We daren't risk damaging a wing squeezing through there. We'll have to fly over. Why don't I go over first and find him? See how thick the wire is. We might be able to leave the girls safely on this side."

"Good idea," whispered Oliver, silencing the girls before they could protest. "But I'll come too. The rest of you wait here. Any problem, fly at once. Don't hang about." Des and Oliver backed a few steps then took a flying leap over the top of the hedge together. As they disappeared the others listened tensely. Emily and Alice were both holding their breath so hard that they felt as though they would burst!

Landing together, Des and Oliver could see the dark outline of a row of cages and sheds a few yards away. They crept to the nearest one and peered through the wire. It seemed to be empty, but in the next one they could see the hunched shape of a large bird roosting on a branch. They looked at one another.

"He might be in there, hiding," whispered Des, pointing to the back of the cage, which was enclosed. "If he's shut in we've got problems."

"I'll risk calling him," Oliver said. He put his nose close to the wire and called softly, "Ollie, Ollie!" There

was a faint rustle from the back of the enclosure. "Ollie, it's me! We've come to get you out!" he said, a little louder, and suddenly there was a scuffling inside and Ollie squeezed himself through a low doorway at the back and rushed towards them.

"Dad, Des…" he choked back tears. "How did you find me? I can't get out. They're taking me to a zoo…"

"Sshh!" said Oliver. "Are you hurt?"

"No, not really. I tried to huff my way out, but the wire's too thick."

Des agreed. "It's pretty strong wire netting. I think it'll need all of us." He clapped a wing to the cage. "No worries, Ollie! I'll fetch the others." Before Ollie could reply he launched himself over the hedge and disappeared.

Oliver looked at his son. "We'll get you out," he said softly. "We won't let you be taken away, I promise."

"Sorry, Dad…" Ollie sniffed, but before he could say any more he gasped as, one by one, Duncan, Emily, Alice, George, Angelica, and finally Des landed outside his cage.

"Ollie!" squealed Alice, much too loudly. Her father shushed her, but not before the eagle in the next cage had woken up. It peered at them suspiciously. None of the dragons noticed him. They clustered round Ollie in delight.

Des began working his way round the netting at the bottom of the cage. "Pretty strong stuff," he said. "Not surprised you couldn't do much with it, Ollie. This'll take some melting! Come on, you lot! Stand back, kids."

Without a word, Duncan, Oliver and George gathered close and breathed fierce jets of flame at one section of wire. They took deep breaths and huffed again. It didn't seem to be having any effect that Emily could see. "Angie!" said Oliver, and without her usual protest she joined them. The wire netting began to smoke and curl under the onslaught of four fiery jets.

"It's working!" breathed Alice. She and Emily began to dance with excitement, but suddenly there was a harsh squawk from the next cage and the eagle flew to the wire.

"What are you up to?" it cried loudly.

"Sshh!!" said Alice and Emily, horrified, and Ollie added, "Please! It's my family! They've come to rescue me!" There were further rustles and cries from further down the line of cages as the birds inside woke up and craned their necks to see what was happening.

The dragons had paused, temporarily out of huff. Ollie pattered to the hole they had made. "It's not big enough!" he said. He tried a huff himself from inside and melted some more.

"Right, girls, come and help!" ordered Oliver. "One last huff, all together. Out of the way Ollie!"

Thrilled, Emily and Alice crept into the middle of the group and they all huffed together. The flame they produced was huge and hot and the wire around the hole began to melt. When they stopped to breathe, Des and Duncan grasped the hot wires and forced them apart. The hole was just big enough, and Ollie, his wings folded tight, crept through.

It was very difficult not to let out a cheer! Alice wanted to give her brother a hug, but High Foured him instead. She beamed, her tears drying on her hot cheeks.

"Let's go!" Oliver cried, preparing to fly over the hedge and away, but Des, who was thoroughly enjoying the night's adventure, stopped him.

"What about that lot?" he said, gesturing at the line of cages.

"What about them?"

"We can't just leave them!" Without waiting for a reply he pattered down the line of cages. "Any of you want out?" he asked.

"Out where?" said a large buzzard. There was a general shaking of wings and rustling of feathers.

"Why would we want to go?" said the eagle. "We get to fly and hunt. It's a good life."

"We're well fed!" added the buzzard, and there was a chorus of agreement. "Why bother?"

Des looked baffled, but a muted shout from Oliver made him shrug his wings and rejoin the others.

"Weird! They want to stay put!" he said, but Oliver didn't wait to hear.

"We're going NOW!" he said firmly. "Before our luck gives out. Over the hedge and back to the tree. Come on!"

They took off and flew across the field. The owl was sitting in the tree finishing off a large rat.

"Well done!" she said, spitting out a beakful of bones and dropping the tail. "You're a lucky young dragon!" she said to Ollie. "You'd have hated the zoo, believe me!"

"I did offer to free the hawks," Des said, "but they didn't want to come!"

"They were hatched in there. They don't know what it's like to be free," said the owl.

"Neither did you when we let you out," said Emily, puzzled.

"We never got to fly, so we reckoned it was worth the risk," said the owl. "I'm off for another rat. Best of luck, all of you-ou-ou…" Her words ended in a hoot as she spread her wings and flew off, to a chorus of thanks from the dragons.

"Better put a few miles between us and those cages before we rest up for the day," said George, and everyone agreed, except Des.

"Pity," he said, looking back as they took off, "I'd like to hide in the hedge and listen to what the Humans say when they find that hole, and no Ollie!"

Chapter 15

Ollie Tells his Tale

It was almost dawn by the time they found a good place to hide and rest for the day. The large copse of trees was so thick and overgrown that even hawks would have found difficulty finding them. They were all weary, but nobody could bear to sleep before they heard Ollie's story, and everyone gathered close, crunching the last of their snacks. Even Angelica seemed eager to listen.

Ollie was still shaky, a pale shadow of his usual boastful self. He took a deep breath and stared at the ground. "I was so fed up at home that I sneaked out of the camp in the middle of the night and thought I'd go south to find Des." His father shook his head in despair. "All right, I know it was stupid, but I couldn't bear the thought of a winter with Aunt Anje!" He attempted a glare at his aunt as he said this, choosing to forget that she had just helped to release him. To Emily's surprise, she looked rather ashamed of herself and didn't protest at his cheek as she usually did.

"Go on," said Oliver. "You obviously didn't get very far."

"No. I found myself flying over that building place you told us about. Those machines you thought were yellow dragons were still there, but I didn't see any Humans, fortunately. But as I went over, a really bright light came on." Duncan and Emily nodded, but didn't interrupt. "It blinded me, and I must have got my direction muddled, because I ended up flying the wrong way – upstream instead of down. By this time it was starting to get light and I needed a place to hide, so I flew on until I spotted that old cave of yours and I crawled in there."

"We thought of that, and Duncan went to look," said Oliver.

"I thought you might, but I was tired so I decided to rest there for a while and then find somewhere else to hide out for the day. I must have fallen asleep, because I was woken up by two big Humans coming into the cave. I kept still, hoping they wouldn't see me, but they shone a light around so they did. They were carrying sticks and sacks. I heard one shout 'Here's one!' and before I could produce a decent huff he hit me on the head so I felt sick and dizzy. They shoved me head-first into a sack and tied it up. I was too squashed to huff without burning myself. I heard one say, 'Any sign of the other one?' and then a few minutes later I was picked up and carried out."

"You and Emily were seen by a Human on the day you flew to the cave," said George. "We found out, and that's why we were so worried. Calm down, son," he added to Oliver, who was starting to huff ominous flames. "Let the lad finish his story!"

"I didn't know about that, or I would never have gone there," Ollie said. "It was awful being carried along in a sack! I wriggled as hard as I could and made a hole with my tail, but they just laughed and put another sack over me as well, so that I could hardly breathe. I thought I would die if it carried on. They must have scrambled down the hill, because

133

there was a lot of slipping and swearing until they threw me down. Then I heard a roar and started to move along faster. It was shoogly, a bit like that train we rode on, but much more bumpy. I was sore all over. After a long time it stopped and I was picked up and carried again. When they let me out of the sack I was in that cage you found me in. I did try a huff then, but it was a bit feeble and they jumped out of the way. My wings were too crumpled to fly. They went outside the cage and shut me in. They stood looking at me and talking, and then they went away. I found there was water, which was a relief, as I was *really* thirsty, but I was terrified! I didn't know what they were going to do to me…" He faltered to a stop, and tears trickled down his face.

His listeners were silent, imagining the horror of it. Alice found herself in tears as well. "You're safe now, Ollie. Tell us the rest of the story after you've had a sleep," George suggested, but Ollie shook his head.

"There isn't much more to tell," he said, sniffing away his tears. "They just came and stared at me. I

heard them say they'd get a lot of money selling me to a zoo. They did feed me, sort of, and I tried to fly to the top of the cage and huff my way out, but the wire was too thick. The bird in the next cage told me not to worry. He said the men were OK, they fed them well and took them out flying. I saw two carried off sitting on huge brown hands. But I hated being stared at, so I hid in the back place. I couldn't huff in there in case I set the straw on fire. I couldn't believe it when I heard Dad and Des outside. Then I worried in case you'd been captured too. I never thought so many of you would come for me. Thank you!"

He gulped and George patted him on the shoulder. "Definitely time to rest!" he said. "You've been very brave, Ollie, but leave the planning to us now. You girls sleep too," he added to Emily and Alice. They were still full of questions, but it was obvious that they would have to wait. Emily tried to stay awake as she heard the grown-ups planning what to do next, but her eyes closed and she fell asleep.

When the children woke up that evening they saw that Sukki and her family had found them. They were full of news. Apparently the men had brought a big crate to transport Ollie to a zoo, and were furious when they found an empty cage. Sukki and her mate had managed a chat to the caged eagle while the men were frantically searching the hedgerows for their missing dragon, and learned of the mass huffing that had finally melted the wire. They were not surprised to learn that the captive birds had refused to be set free. "Can't understand it mesel', but they seem to like living there," Sukki's mate said. They left a farewell gift of pigeons and departed for their night's roost, waved away by the grateful dragons.

"Does Mum know we've found Ollie?" Alice asked anxiously, and heard that Duncan and Oliver had signalled home to say that Ollie was safe, and a very relieved Ellen was looking forward to welcoming him home. Duncan and Oliver, with Ollie and the girls, were to start for home that night. Emily hoped that Des would be coming too, but she was disappointed.

"I'm going south to see George and Angie safely to this place of hers," he said. "I might stay a day or so, if that's all right with you, Anje?" Alice choked on her cold nettle tea on hearing her usually haughty aunt addressed like this, but to her surprise Angelica only simpered and said again that he'd be welcome. "Then I'll come up north to join you," Des continued. "There's still plenty of time before the winter sets in. But it's no good thinking you can camp out in Scotland all winter, Ollie. And no more trying to go solo! I don't want to spend the rest of my life rescuing you." He gave Ollie a friendly buffet with his wing to show he wasn't too serious, and then turned to George and Angelica. "Can we get started? Might as well make the most of the night."

Des and George began to collect Angelica's luggage, and to their surprise, she picked some up too. Emily wondered if she might have become a reformed character, especially when she turned to Ollie and Oliver and said, "I believe it was partly my fault that you ran away, Ollie. It was very disobedient of you of course, but I'm sorry if I caused the trouble. I hope

I'll see you all in a few weeks, and dear Ellen and the baby too. We'll have rooms in the castle all ready for you, won't we, Desmond?" She fluttered her eyelashes at him and Emily and Alice tried not to laugh at his horrified look. George winked at them again.

It was now fully dark and Des judged it was safe to depart. The three dragons rose in the air and set off south, and the others waved until they were out of sight.

"I'm going to miss Grandad," said Alice sadly.

"Me too," said Ollie, unexpectedly. Emily glanced at him, wondering if his adventures would have changed him. He was not going to forget his capture and imprisonment in a hurry. She shuddered at the thought of it.

"But we won't miss old Angie! Even if she does seem to be a bit nicer now," she said, trying to cheer them up. "It'll be nice to have our tree-house back."

"As long as it doesn't still smell of perfume!" said Ollie, sounding a bit more like his old self. Oliver grinned and clapped him on the back with a wing.

"I think life by the loch might be more peaceful without her. And we'll see George again soon," he added. "We can enjoy the autumn together before we have to go. Now, are you all fit to fly home?"

The children nodded eagerly. "Good," said Duncan, spreading his wings. "I think there are a few dragons waiting in a cave for the wanderers to return! Let's see if we can get back to our glen before the sun comes up."

They soared together into the night sky.

END OF BOOK FOUR

Winter is difficult for Scottish Dragons, and this is a particularly hard one. Emily and Tom are missing their friends. A new game on the frozen loch with the otters is fun for a while, but soon they are trapped and in danger.

Help is needed, and it comes from an unexpected person!

A dangerous journey, a secret hide-out, and the closest encounter yet with Humans make this the most adventurous of the Dragon Tales so far...

Find out more in *Dragon Tales Book V: Dragons in Snow* by Judy Hayman, coming soon.

NEW! Dragon Tales Colouring Book

Coming soon, a selection of Caroline Wolfe Murray's lovely illustrations enlarged for you to colour and keep. 40 pages of beautiful pictures, with information about the dragons and their adventures.

For more information on these or any of the Dragon Tales titles, contact Practical Inspiration Publishing: info@alisonjones.com.

Acknowledgements

As always, thanks to Alison and Caroline, without whom these books would still be in my head.

To my five grandchildren, Phoebe, Elise, David, Sam and Megan, who continue to be enthusiastic about this book project, despite their advancing years. They are full of so many good ideas that I have yet to use them all, and will have to keep on writing. This time, thanks especially to Phoebe, for inventing Aunt Angelica and her handbag several years ago.

To my good supportive friends and the rest of my family, for their tolerance and promotional skills. Especially to Alison A, who first had the idea of a colouring book, and Kitty, whose class tops the league.

And to all the lively children and their teachers that I meet on school visits, who send me letters, drawings and lots of ideas.

About the Author

Judy Hayman lives with her husband Peter on the edge of the Lammermuir Hills in East Lothian, Scotland, where there is a wonderful view and plenty of wildlife, but no dragons, as far as she knows. At various times in her past life she has taught English in a big comprehensive school; written plays, directed and occasionally acted for amateur theatre companies; been a Parliamentary candidate for both Westminster and the Scottish Parliament; and a Mum. Sometimes all at once. Now preventing the Lammermuirs from taking over her garden, being a Gran, writing more Dragon Tales and visiting schools to talk about them takes up a lot of her time.

About the Illustrator

Caroline Wolfe Murray studied Archaeology at the University of Edinburgh and took a career path in the field, turning her hand to archaeological illustration. She has always had a passion for exploration and discovery which evolved from her experience of living in Spain, Belgium, Venezuela and New Zealand. She now resides in East Lothian with her husband James and her two young daughters Lily and Mabel, who have been her inspiration to work on a children's book.

Read on for the first chapter of Dragon Tales Book V: Dragons in Snow, *coming soon...*

Chapter 1

Goodbye until Spring!

Emily the dragon sat on the landing branch of the tree-house that she had built so happily with Tom, Alice and Ollie earlier in the summer. It had been the best summer ever, especially their seaside adventure with Des! But now every bit of her was drooping miserably: wings, ears, tail, talons. Two tears slithered down her scales and dripped down her neck. Even her spikes felt limp. She couldn't even manage a final wave as the tiny flying shapes of her friends disappeared into the distance on their way south for the winter.

A silence fell.

Down below, her Mum, Dad and younger brother Tom had been waving and shouting goodbye, while baby Lily bounced and huffed in excitement, not understanding what all the fuss was about. But now they all turned to look up at the sad heap of Emily, just visible in the gathering dusk. She didn't want to talk to anybody. She pushed her way through the bracken doorway and buried herself as deep as she could into the pile of left-over heather on the floor.

"Leave her alone for a while," Gwen said to Tom, who was about to fly up to the branch. "She'll cheer up! Why don't you help us clear up the last bits of their camp and then we can go home."

"It looks clear enough to me," said Tom, miserably. He wasn't as upset as Emily, but he wasn't looking forward to a winter without the excitements that Ollie and Des could provide.

"We mustn't leave any trace, remember?" said Duncan. "You never know when Humans might come snooping. You rough up that flattened grass with your tail while we pack up these things to store in the cave." Tom set to work, while his father collected all the remaining firewood from the camp and tied a neat bundle with an ivy strand.

When they had finished, there was still no sign of Emily.

"You go on, and take Lily," Gwen said. "Get the fire going and supper ready. It's going to be a cold night." She gathered the remaining heather from the beds in the camp and flew to the landing branch with it. She sighed sympathetically as she peered in at the quivering heap on the floor, and wondered how she could cheer her daughter up. It wasn't going to be easy!

Buried in her heather, and still sobbing, Emily was remembering the last few weeks with Alice and Ollie. After the dramatic rescue of Ollie from the Humans' cage, she and Alice, with Ollie and the Dads, had flown back home to a wonderful welcome. She pictured Tom as she had seen him, dancing and cheering on top of Ben McIlwhinnie's bald head as they flew in, and then Ellen hugging her son – who didn't seem to mind, to

Emily's surprise – and Georgie and Lily getting under everybody's claws. And how they took turns to tell the tale of the search and rescue and the help the Hawks and Owls had given, while they devoured the hot supper that had been waiting for them. And how proud she and Alice had been as the Dads told about the parts they had played. And how they all fell silent and huddled a little closer together round the fire as Ollie had told how he had been captured and imprisoned. She still shuddered when she remembered that awful cage and the sight of a miserable and frightened Ollie inside it. It had taken seven of them to huff a hole in the wire big enough for him to escape.

Then, ten days later, there had been the excitement of Des returning, as he had promised, to tell how he had escorted Old George and Aunt Angelica to her famous Castle, and had a good snoop round before making the journey back. "It's a pretty good place she's found," he had reported. "Near to Human settlements, but well hidden. There's a high fence all round, and pretty dense woodland. She's got good stores of food and plenty of room."

So sadly everything had been decided! Ellen, Oliver and the children would fly south to spend the winter in the castle, and Des would go too, to show them the way, and perhaps to stay himself during the worst of the weather. He comforted Alice and Ollie with the thought that there was room enough for them to keep well out of Angie's way, and even Ollie had to agree that it was the only thing to do. His adventure, when he narrowly escaped a zoo, seemed to have made him a good deal more sensible, though Alice and Emily both wondered if it would last.

But none of these memories helped Emily now. There had been two happy weeks before they left, the departure delayed by three days of high wind which had stripped the last of the leaves and warned of bad weather to come. The children had enjoyed the wind, laughing and tumbling in the air, playing complicated chasing games, but finally, yesterday, it had dropped. The air turned colder, and Des insisted it was time to go.

As usual, they set off in the gloaming to fly at night and hide by day, and now that they had gone, Emily had to face a lonely winter.

Sniffing, she realised that her mother had come in quietly and was sitting on the floor beside her heap of heather.

"I know, Emily, it's hard for you and Tom! You've had a lovely summer, and a lot of excitement. But it won't be as bad as you think. They've promised to come back in the spring. And Tom's growing up. He was a lot more sensible while you were away looking for Ollie, even though he was disappointed not to go with you. He'll miss Ollie and Alice as well. You'll manage, with him, and Lily, and your books. Didn't you swap one with Alice before she left? So that's a new story you have! Come on, the supper will be burning."

Emily knew she couldn't stay buried forever. Slowly she emerged, damp, miserable and covered in bits. Her mother smiled sympathetically. "Let's go home," she said, holding out a talon.

Emily sighed deeply. "I suppose I am a bit hungry…" she admitted. They flew back to the cave together.

Mum was right when she said that Tom was growing up, Emily thought, as she ate her crow and toadstool hotpot. In the past he would have laughed at her for crying, but this time he didn't and after the hotpot was finished, he even offered her the last dried rosehip and helped to clear up without complaining. When they had finished, they sat for a while in the firelight, and the stars shone bright and clear. The moon was a thin crescent low on the horizon.

"It's a perfect night for their flight," said Gwen, coming out after putting Lily to bed and speaking of their absent friends for the first time. "I hope they manage to find a good safe spot to hide during the day tomorrow."

"Des knows all the good places," said Duncan. "They'll be fine. He'll find them a hidden spot where they can sleep. I wonder if he'll stay with them all winter."

"Des never stays anywhere for long," said Tom. "Perhaps he'll come back here."

"No, he won't do that. He knows we've only just enough space and food to keep the five of us going until the spring. What we must do now is make sure we're ready for the winter ourselves. You two will have plenty to keep you occupied, don't worry. Firewood and foraging tomorrow! No time to brood."

"OK," said Tom, before Emily could reply. "Bags I do berries."

"No chance. You always eat as many as you save!" his Dad teased him.

Emily began to feel better. Perhaps her mother was right about Tom. She heaved a deep sigh, her huff smoky in the cold air. "I think I'll go to bed and read Alice's book," she said. "Come on, Tom, it's getting cold out here."

Their parents smiled at each other as Tom and Emily disappeared.

"They'll be all right," said Gwen.

"And I reckon the others got away just in time," said Duncan thoughtfully. "There's going to be a frost tonight. Winter's here!"

"And earlier than usual! I think these last foraging days might be important, if our food's to last. Emily and Tom have bigger appetites these days, and we used up such a lot of food when the others came for meals."

"It might be time to try that roots idea that Oliver told me about," said Duncan thoughtfully as he banked up the fire with turf to keep it burning gently until morning.

His wife snorted. "I don't think a bit of digging will cheer the kids up. Better think of something more exciting if we're to survive the winter!"

For more information on the Dragon Tales books, email info@alisonjones.com.

Lightning Source UK Ltd.
Milton Keynes UK
UKHW021254251119
354201UK00007B/527/P